Russell Evans

SURVIVAL

PUFFIN BOOKS

Puffin Books, Penguin Books Ltd, Harmondsworth,
Middlesex, England
Penguin Books, 625 Madison Avenue,
New York, New York 10022, U.S.A.
Penguin Books Australia Ltd, Ringwood,
Victoria, Australia
Penguin Books Canada Ltd, 2801 John Street,
Markham, Ontario, Canada L3R 1B4
Penguin Books (N.Z.) Ltd, 182-190 Wairau Road,
Auckland 10, New Zealand

—

First published by Dobson Books Ltd 1979
Published in Puffin Books 1981

—

Copyright © Russell Evans, 1979
All rights reserved

—

Printed in Great Britain by
Cox & Wyman Ltd, Reading
Set in Monophoto Baskerville

—

SURVIVAL

'Let us in, please let us in,' wailed the men outside, clutching frantically at the wire of the gates.

Ivanov had known them before their escape, but now he couldn't recognise them. Hair and beards long and matted, clothes hanging in tatters on skeletal bodies. 'Just like scarecrows,' he whispered.

'They were fools to come back,' replied Rogojin. 'Better if they'd died free men out in the woods. At least you've a chance in the taiga. You're up against nature, not man. There's hope out there, none here.'

Later, Ivanov took his chance and made his break from the Siberian prison camp. Only then did he discover just how slender the hope of survival was. Narrowly evading his pursuers, he was forced to run and run. Unable to rest, weakening with every mile, he was up against the primary law of the wild: kill or be killed.

Developing the skills and instincts of a wild animal, Ivanov's will to live looked as though it would triumph ... until a secret carried in a crashed aeroplane brought with it a danger more deadly than nature ever devised.

Relentless suspense and a marvellously authentic background make *Survival* a powerful and absorbing novel for readers of eleven and over. It was commended in the 1979 *Guardian* fiction awards.

Part One

THE ESCAPE

I

It was not until the fifteen who had escaped in the Spring came back and knelt in the snow at the gates, crying piteously to be let in, that Ivanov really understood how cruel the taiga could be in winter.

'Poor bastards,' he muttered from the side of his mouth.

'Don't waste your sympathy,' Rogojin muttered back. 'They're to blame for this special muster. We'll freeze to death on their account.'

No snow was falling, but a searching wind from the north made eddies of white dust rise from the hard-packed snow of the mustering ground. The prisoners, lined up in three ranks, stamped their feet cautiously, one eye on the guards.

Ivanov looked again at the fifteen men huddled together outside the camp's high, barbed-wire gates.

'It's the cold that beat them,' he said, adding wonderingly, 'to think that they're just busting to get back in here again – into this hell hole. That means the taiga must be really terrible.'

'Not so terrible as this,' grunted Rogojin. He was hugging his armpits against the cold, and without withdrawing his hands he raised his elbows to indicate the wooden watchtowers, the perimeter fence, the rows of mean huts. 'There's just nothing viler than this....'

'Quiet!' shouted a guard, his harsh Tartar voice rising

above the shuffling and muttering of the prisoners. In the sudden silence the voices of the men outside came clear on the wind.

'Let us in, please let us in,' they wailed, clutching frantically at the wire of the gates. Some still strong enough to shout, called to guards they knew by name.

'Comrade Memel, it's me, your old trusty Andrey. Please open the gate. Punish me for the fool I've been, but please let me in.'

Ivanov had known these men before their escape, but now he couldn't recognise them. Hair and beards long and matted, clothes hanging in tatters on skeletal bodies. 'Just like scarecrows,' he whispered to Rogojin. 'And I bet you anything Cousin Khan won't let them in.'

Ivanov was right, for the Commandant, big as a bear in his greatcoat, had now arrived at the gate and was standing, legs stiffly apart, mittened hands on hips, looking at the men outside, every line of his huge figure conveying the contempt he felt for them.

Abruptly he swung on his heels to face the paraded prisoners.

'See how they come crawling back!' he bawled. 'They were brave enough fellows, weren't they, when they escaped in the Spring, but what d'you think of 'em now, eh?'

He turned to face the gate again. 'You out there,' he taunted, 'you'd like to resume your holiday with me? But for the winter only, of course. You'll be off again, come the Spring. Is that it, you oafs?'

'No, no, Comrade Commandant!' they shouted back, panic in their voices. 'We promise we won't run off again.'

'In that case,' the Commandant bellowed unctuously, 'I'll see what reservations I can make for you – in the punishment block. But I'm too busy to attend to it now. You'll have to wait out there until tomorrow.'

With that he marched stiffly off, paying no heed to the

chorus of anguish which rose from the men outside the gates.

'I can't see them surviving the night,' whispered Ivanov.

'They were fools to come back,' replied Rogojin. 'Better if they'd died free men out in the woods. At least you've a chance in the taiga. You're up against nature, not man. There's hope out there, none here.'

Rogojin paused for breath. Seven years in the camp had left him bronchial and arthritic, an old man in his early thirties.

'I'd make a break for it if I could,' he wheezed. 'But I'm not strong enough now, I've left it too late!'

He moved closer, his lips almost touching Ivanov's cheek. 'Don't make my mistake, Ivan. Get out when you're still strong, and stay out. You could do it, I know you could.'

Ivanov was surprised. 'Me?' he said. 'You know me – a four-thumbed schoolmaster who couldn't make a fire or skin a rabbit to save his life. You must be mad.'

Rogojin shook his head. 'You've got the brains, lad, you've got the guts and you're strong enough. Those lads out there were strong all right, but they didn't have the head you've got. They thought they knew everything. You know you know nothing. That's a start that'll take you far in the taiga.'

This was nonsense, thought Ivanov. He was the least likely of all the camp's inmates to beat the taiga. Even so, it was nice to be told he could make it. Poor old Rogojin. His fever was making him light-headed....

2

That night Ivanov couldn't get to sleep. Usually he was so tired after the day's labour that sleep came like a blow as soon as he had crawled into his bunk. But not that night. He couldn't rid his mind of Rogojin's hoarse whispering – 'Escape! You've got the brains, the guts....!'

Indeed, why not escape? Rogojin wasn't as mad as all that when he talked about using brains. Other break-outs had failed for want of forethought.

Plan ahead, leave as little as possible to chance – that was the formula for success, decided Ivanov. Like the others he'd have to make his break-out in the Spring – the climate dictated that – but unlike them he'd purposefully prepare for the winter ahead, that first winter which would test to the uttermost his ability to survive. Everything depended on that first winter.

'If I get through it,' he mused, 'I could then continue south the following Spring, holing up again for another winter, then south again the Spring after that. I could cover hundreds of miles that way, hundreds – why, I could even walk in on Katerina and little Alyosha. What a wonderful surprise they'd have–'

Ivanov stiffened in his bunk, fists clenched. He must not daydream like that. He must not even think of his wife and boy. They were not just hundreds and hundreds of miles away, they were ten years away – the ten years of his sentence.

He lay listening to the night sounds of the hut, the snores, the uneasy stirrings of his comrades, the muttered, unintelligible snatches of sleep-talk. This was their only freedom, to lie abed and dream. Their every waking moment was taken up with back-breaking labour which left them in a stupor of exhaustion. Food was all they could think of, and what food they got! Watery skilly, with rare fragments of potato floating in it, and a hunk of hard, black bread.

No wonder Rogojin was always ill. Only the strongest could survive that killing regimen, day after day, year after year. Would he, too, become like Rogojin?

That was when Ivanov decided to escape. Better to die in the woods than become a decrepit shadow of himself, he argued. Better that Katerina should remember him as he was now than see him ten years hence, a shell of the man she knew.

And what had Rogojin said? 'At least there's hope out there in the taiga.' Hope, no matter how frail. A chance to survive, albeit so slender. Why should he deny himself his daydream?

3

Next morning Ivanov's hut was detailed for timber felling, and by watching how the guards paired off the prisoners he managed to get Rogojin as his mate on one of the big saws.

'Thanks,' grinned Rogojin. 'The others don't fancy having me on one end of a saw. They think I'm not strong enough now to keep up with them and they'll fall short on the norm.'

'To hell with the norm,' said Ivanov. 'I can pull and push for both of us. You take it easy and listen.'

He looked round. The nearest guard was well beyond hearing and the nearest pair of prisoners had already started sawing, keeping time with a rhythmically murmured 'In, out – in, out.'

'When Spring comes I'm making a break for it.'

Rogojin released his end of the saw and sat back, his haunches in the snow, his ravaged features showing a surprised delight.

'Good for you, boy, good for you! I'll help you all I can. We'll make this a real escape, the first this camp has ever had.'

It was his turn now to look round. Reassured, he gripped the handle of the saw again and feebly pushed and pulled, leaving the real labour to Ivanov on the other end. The tall spruce they were sawing shuddered gently and let fall wispy trails of frozen snow.

'First thing is fire. I've got a piece of flint and the broken end of a steel file stowed away. I'll show you how to make a spark by striking the flint on the file. Tinder is important, too. You'll have to have a water-tight pouch of some sort to keep dried pine needles in – and some cones, too. Both are full of resin and will kindle from a spark....'

Rogojin's eyes were shining, and not from fever this time, thought Ivanov. But he said nothing, listening carefully as his friend expertly listed what had to be done.

'An axe is essential and it shouldn't be too difficult to pick up an axe-head between now and the Spring. You've got a knife, haven't you?'

Ivanov nodded. It was an old bread knife, of the sort with a serrated blade, and the blade had broken short only two inches from the handle. He had filed away the saw edge and whetted the steel until it was razor sharp.

'Then we have to find something for you to hunt with. Wire is no problem. That's for snares, of course, and I'll show you how to make one so that you can bag some hares. We can make a line and hooks for fishing. That's again easy. But a weapon for fair-sized game is the problem....'

Rogojin paused, his brows creased in an expressive frown, looking so elaborately puzzled that Ivanov had to laugh.

'Stop kidding,' he said. 'You've thought all this out a thousand times.'

Rogojin smiled back. 'A bow and arrow,' he said, 'that's the answer. There's the right wood for the picking round here to make a bow with. And we could tip the arrows with bits of metal, even if it's only boot nails.'

'But I'm no Red Indian!' exploded Ivanov. 'Using a bow and arrow needs a lot of skill. How the devil am I going to get the practice?'

'As you go along,' said Rogojin. 'Right from the first day you make your break you start practising.'

His voice was grim now. 'You said yourself you were four-thumbed. You've never set a snare, nor fished, nor hunted. Any country kid knows more about life in the woods than you. So once you're outside, you've got to learn fast, real fast....'

4

He'd done it! Ivanov, gasping for breath, crouched in a thicket of birch and listened to his pursuers. Their shouted commands, still muffled by distance, seemed nearer now. They'd found his trail and were following it.

He set off again at a steady lope. 'Easy does it,' he told himself, though his heart was racing, his mouth dry with threatening panic. Rogojin had told him not to run in speedy spurts but keep up a regular jog trot. 'They'll seem to be gaining on you at times, but don't let that bother you.'

Easier said than done, thought Ivanov. He skirted an

area of swamp where the Spring thaw had made a shallow lake, pausing as he did so to check his bearings. It was important to keep going dead straight otherwise he'd circle back on his pursuers.

His detour to avoid the swamp brought him into an abandoned clearing where a tangle of young birch and larch suddenly slowed him to a walk. This was the sort of terrain Rogojin had warned him against. 'Avoid secondary growth, it's too thick to get through quickly. Make a track through old forest.'

But how was he to tell what lay ahead? It had all sounded so simple back in the camp. In fact, neither he nor Rogojin had anticipated such a close pursuit; their main worry had been the actual break-out. And that had turned out to be almost laughably easy. Ivanov had literally walked to his freedom.

He'd been on a working party outside the camp, making a clearing in the woods for what was to be a new sawmill. Rogojin had feigned a fit – as old a trick as prison itself – but it had worked long enough to distract the attention of the guards, and long enough for Ivanov to slip from tree to tree into the shadows of the forest.

He stopped again to listen for his pursuers. They had reached the edge of the swamp and to judge by their shouts were spreading out around it. Ivanov glanced up at the sky. One advantage of being in the clearing was to get direction from the sun, and he was delighted to find it high to his left. That meant he had made steady progress south.

He suddenly groped at his body, feeling his legs and then his shoulders like a man exploring for broken bones. He sighed with relief. All was safely secured beneath his clothing – the arrows lashed to his shins, the axe-head tied to his belt and the bow strapped to his shoulders.

He moved deeper into the clearing, forcing his way through the whip-like growth of the young birches, stumbling over trunks of larch, felled long ago and left to rot. He was fighting for breath now and wondered how long he could keep going at this pace.

When he at last reached high trees again their shade came so abruptly that for a moment he thought a cloud had blotted out the sun. He wiped the sweat from his eyes with a sleeve and looked carefully ahead. There was pine mixed with fir and spruce to his left, more birch and larch to his right.

'I'm learning fast,' he said to himself grimly, and headed for the pines, breaking into a gentle trot which felt effortless after his hectic scramble through the clearing.

The ground was spongy underfoot, centuries of cone and needle compressed into an ash-brown carpet. Water was everywhere: dripping from the trees, running in rivulets between the trunks, forming shallow pools. Ivanov knew this was the aftermath of the thaw. In only a matter of days the forest would become dry – never bone dry, for the ground was too frost-bound for the water to seep deeply, and there was little evaporation in the chill gloom of these woods.

He ran on at a steady trot, weaving his way in and out of the trees, glancing up now and then to catch a glimpse of the sky. Where it was lightest he judged the sun to be. He realised this was crude navigation, but it kept him moving roughly south.

'And I'm not wasting time looking for moss growing on the sheltered side of trees,' he reflected, grinning as he recalled Rogojin's explosive dismissal of that theory. 'What absolute rubbish!' he had declaimed. 'Trees in the middle of a forest are not exposed to wind from any fixed direction. If there's moss you'll find it growing evenly up the trunk on all sides. To find a tree with moss growing up one side only, you must find the exposed edge of the forest – and how the hell d'you do that when you're in the middle of it?'

He stopped once and scrambled up the close-branched

trunk of a tall spruce. From his lofty perch he listened for sounds of pursuit. 'They've turned back,' he muttered to himself, suppressing a sudden surge of glee which made him want to shout his triumph to the tree tops. Could he be sure?

5

Resolving not to take any chances, Ivanov walked on at a brisk pace, not stopping until nightfall found him at the edge of an immense clearing.

It was a natural clearing, made by a forest fire which had scythed its way through the taiga, reducing the trees to blackened stumps. And the soil between the stumps, freed from the eternal shade of foliage and able to breath now that its suffocating carpet of needles had been burnt to ash, had erupted in lush grass and berrying shrubs, some of which were already in flower.

Ivanov knew what to do – thanks to Rogojin. He knelt to put himself at eye level with the grass, already some six inches high. There was still sufficient light for him to detect the delicate track left by hares – an almost imperceptible bending of the grass.

He pulled his shirt out from his trousers and unwound a length of fine wire which was around his waist. He wrenched a thin branch off a pine and, using his precious bread knife, swiftly whittled two pegs. In a matter of minutes he had fixed a snare on one of the hare trails.

Carefully he back-tracked to the edge of the clearing, to the spot where he had emerged from the woods. He would camp down there for the night, he decided. But first he must make a shaft for his axe-head.

He wandered among the trees until he found a spruce bough of the right girth. It was too thick to wrench off by hand, so he stood on it and stamped it off. He whittled the thicker end to fit the axe-head and rammed it home, using a charred tree stump as an anvil.

He balanced the finished tool in his hand and smiled ruefully. It was a rough job, but with it he could fashion a finer shaft later on.

Using the axe he chopped off the lower boughs of a young fir and made a bed of the soft foliage, arranging it at the foot of a low growing pine which would provide shelter from the frost.

He then rolled up his trouser legs and removed the arrows bound to his shins. From his right thigh he removed a canvas satchel and fastened it securely to his belt. The satchel carried his flint and tinder, but he'd not risk a fire that night.

He took off his shirt and carefully unhitched the bow from his shoulder. It had been unstrung and Rogojin had fastened it so that its length reached from his right shoulder down into the top of his right trouser leg.

It was a neatly wrought weapon, made of seasoned yew, with a fine wire string and a tension screw. How Rogojin had obtained the materials Ivanov could not guess, but he knew the delight his friend had taken in making the bow. Would it work, he wondered – or, more to the point – would he, four-thumbed Ivan, be able to make it work?

He'd start practising as soon as he was on his way next day; meanwhile, he'd settle down for the night. With that thought he removed his trousers – but not with the intention of sleeping without them. Neatly stitched to the inside of the seat was a blanket. Old Rogojin thought of everything!

Finally he groped inside his canvas satchel and

removed three hunks of bread. They were a dirty grey and mildewed, but the sight of them made his stomach lurch. In the excitement of the day he'd forgotten his hunger.

Should he eat one hunk now, or two – or all three? He steadied himself. This bread was his only food until he'd trapped or shot down something with his bow. One piece it would have to be.

Next morning Ivanov was up before the sun, searching in the grey light for his snare. It wasn't where he'd set it, but feeling in the grass for the pegs he found the wire and pulled it towards him. It was heavy. Caught in the noose was a fat hare.

For a moment he didn't know what to do: shout with joy or weep. But he felt he had to thank somebody, so he thanked the dead hare, stroking the soft, white fur of its head.

As he knelt the sun's rim peeped above the horizon, sending out a wave of pink across the sky, flushing the sombre greys and greens of the wilderness with a warm glow.

Ivanov gasped. He had seen these spectacular dawns of the far north often enough from within the prison camp. But now he was deeply moved. This was his first red dawn as a free man, and he saw it as a promise of freedom, of life – if only for one day more.

'Wise is the man in the wilderness,' Rogojin had said, 'who counts his life in days. . . .'

6

Though he could detect no sign nor sound of pursuit Ivanov decided not to delay his departure by skinning the hare. He would do that later – and carefully, for the hide of the little creature could be as important to him as the meat.

'Whatever you kill, skin carefully,' Rogojin had told him. 'Your prison boots will only last you fifty miles and you'll need every strip of hide you can get for making moccasins.'

Ivanov wrapped the hare round his neck, tying its legs under his chin, and with the prospect of a hot meal of meat at the end of the day, he set off at a brisk pace.

By sunset he was confident he had covered more than thirty miles, but he decided to press on. Though the sun was down, the onrush of Spring was pushing back the night and he could still see well enough, even in the gloom of the forest, to walk many miles more.

And that was almost his undoing. In the misty half light he didn't see the men until he heard their whispering. He flung himself to the ground, hardly believing that he in turn had not been seen.

They were not more than thirty feet from him, squatting in a rough circle, their backs to trees, and arguing.

'No fire!' one of them whispered fiercely. 'No fire, and that's that. And no noise, either. A peep out of any of you and I'll have you skinned alive.'

There was a murmur of protest, followed by a whispered question which Ivanov failed to hear.

'No doubt about it,' replied the same voice, strained into hoarseness. 'He kipped down last night, that was his first mistake so far, and now we're ahead of him and he doesn't know it. We'll stay here spread out, a hundred yards between each man. And so long as we keep quiet we'll hear him come blundering through. No matter how far away he is we'll hear him all right.'

Ivanov became suddenly aware of the silence. The man was right. The incessant wind, as much part of the taiga as the very trees, had dropped. His footsteps had been muffled by the soft litter of the woods, but a cough, a muttered curse, even the swish of his clothing could have been heard for a hundred yards or more. He was lucky: their whispering had drowned the sound of his approach.

'How are you sure he'll come this way? There's no end to this forest, Alexis, just no end...' The tired whisper trailed off on a note of despair, and Ivanov guessed that his pursuers' night-long trek without sleep was taking its toll.

'Don't worry, he's sure to come this way.' Ivanov now recognised the speaker. It was Alexis Petrisky, a guard from the camp who had worked for years in the woods, an expert hunter and trapper.

'He's heading south,' continued Petrisky, 'south like a swallow, dead on course, yet keeping to open woods to make good time. Couldn't do better myself.' There was grudging admiration in Petrisky's voice.

'But there's one thing the poor slob doesn't know. Marshy scrub closes in here, making this stretch of woods into a sort of bottleneck. He'll walk right into us.'

Ivanov pressed closer to the ground. He hadn't counted on the guards keeping up the pursuit as far as this. There were perhaps fifteen of them, though in the patchy twilight he could make out only vague forms and there could have been more.

'Right, get to your stations!' At Petrisky's command the men shuffled off to left and right, disappearing in the quickening gloom. Ivanov's heart sank. If Petrisky remained where he was there'd be no escape. It would be fatal to move a muscle.

But at that moment a sound filled the forest behind Ivanov, a vast rustling which brought Petrisky to his feet with a curse. It was rain, Ivanov realised, a cloudburst spewing water on the taiga. As it hit them the gloom of late twilight deepened into sudden night, and Ivanov was on his feet, feeling his way from tree to tree, knowing that any noise he made would be drowned in the din of the downpour.

His first impulse was to return the way he had come, but he realised he must move forward so as to get ahead of his pursuers. He gave the place where he'd last seen Petrisky a wide berth and then began to run, arms outstretched like a blind man.

Crashing painfully into unseen trees, his face rasped by branches, his shins barked by fallen logs, Ivanov continued his mad sprint until he judged himself to be well clear of Petrisky. He then settled down to a fast walk, vowing not to stop until he'd left his pursuers far behind.

7

That was the start of a mammoth trek. Cutting down his sleeping time to a minimum he slogged steadily through the lengthening days and was confident at the end of a week that he had covered more than 200 miles. But it had cost him dear.

His boots were in tatters, his feet a mass of broken blisters, and lean though he was to start with, his suddenly sharp shins, protruding ribs, forearms like sticks, told him he had lost every ounce of superfluous flesh. If he was to keep up his strength he must, he realised, replace that flesh. From now on hunting, not walking, had to be the order of his day.

That hare, trapped on his first night in the woods, had long been eaten – to the last shred of muscle and gut. Following Rogojin's instructions he had cut the meat into thin slivers which he grilled lightly over a small fire of pine cones. He had then packed away the meat in his satchel – his hard tack for the march ahead. And not only had the charred meat remained appetisingly wholesome, but it had sustained him for the first four days.

His stomach contracted with hunger as he recalled what

he had done with the remainder of the hare – the heart, lungs, kidney, liver, intestines. It had all gone into his 'pot', the prison-issue pannikin which had never been so richly filled before. Rarely had he tasted such stew; it had literally poured strength into him – a hot, glutinous stream of pure protein.

Ivanov groaned. That was seven days ago and since then his only luck had been to catch a quite pathetic morsel – a young and very small suslik, or ground squirrel.

He had stopped for a ten-minute break and was seated with his back to a tree when the suslik popped up out of its hole – right between his legs. With a reflex honed by hunger Ivanov's hand shot out like a striking snake and the tiny rodent died in his grip without even a squeak.

Ivanov felt vaguely ashamed. This was not the hunting he had imagined. But even so, he dissected the creature with care, eating all but bladder and bowels and – as with the hare – carefully scraping the hide and storing it in his satchel. When he'd found his winter quarters he would stretch and dry the skins. Even the suslik's might make half a glove!

That had been two days before and now Ivanov faced another night on an agonisingly empty stomach. He collected dead wood for a fire and sat huddled over the blaze, not caring now if the light alerted his pursuers.

'If you're out there,' he suddenly shouted, 'come and get me, Alexis Petrisky. I'll trade this sort of freedom for a tin of your meat.'

The echo of his voice startled him and he scrambled hurriedly to his feet, legs trembling, heart pounding. A nauseating giddiness brought him to his knees, but he rose again, slowly this time, and began to kick at the fire, stamping on the embers.

He realised he was much weaker than he'd thought when he'd stopped for the night. He crawled to the base of a pine, wrapped his blanket tightly round him and sat with his back against the tree, peering anxiously into the encircling gloom of the taiga.

He cursed himself for having started such a big fire. While he was fairly certain the guards from the camp had given up the chase he felt uneasy about Petrisky. The old hunter might keep doggedly on his track long after the others had turned back.

But hunger might get him before Petrisky, he reflected gloomily. He couldn't walk any more without food, that was certain. He must stay where he was and start hunting game in earnest.

His first task at dawn, he determined, was to find a clearing with grass, and lay more snares. While waiting for a catch he could practice with Rogojin's bow. He had already tried it out and found he couldn't hit a tree at five paces, but that was his fault, not Rogojin's. Properly handled the bow could become a weapon of rare precision, and it shot the arrows with astonishing velocity – hard and fast enough to bring down one of the small deer of the taiga.

Comforted by the thought that he was still capable of at least planning a day of action, his tenseness left him and he drifted into sleep, his hunger cramps for the moment stilled....

8

Suddenly he was awake. Something furry had brushed against his face. Wolverine or bear? His flesh crept. Then he heard a chittering and rustling in the trees above him. It was squirrels, not just one or two, but hundreds.

In the grey light of early dawn he could see them wriggling along the branches, jumping from tree to tree.

As he watched, three clambered down the trunk he'd been leaning against and bounded across the forest floor.

It was a migration. Rogojin had told him about it. Obeying a mysterious, primeval urge the red squirrels would start moving, in small bands to begin with, their numbers multiplying as others were attracted to their headlong rush until hundreds or even a thousand might be seen scampering through the woods.

Ivanov could hardly believe his good fortune. He was in the middle of a moving feast of meat! He snatched his axe-shaft from his belt (he carried the axe-head separately in his satchel for safety) and lashed out at the squirrels as they leapt and plunged about his feet. In no time he'd killed more than a dozen.

Pausing for breath he noticed that a stand of pine some fifty feet away seemed festooned in the little creatures. And then he realised why. It was Cembra, the pine Rogojin had so carefully described and which he'd been on the look-out for each day of his trek. It bore cones which were particularly favoured by squirrels, and – much more important than that – the seed in the cones could be eaten by man.

With a shout Ivanov ran to the Cembras and with the axe-shaft beat a tattoo on the trunks of the trees. He was afraid that so many squirrels would strip the trees bare of cones. But he need not have worried. Such was their haste to move on that the squirrels had time for no more than a quick nibble, discarding the cones almost as soon as they had bitten them free of the branches.

Ivanov could hardly restrain his glee as the cones rained down on his upturned face. The squirrels were doing his garnering for him!

For some time after the squirrels had gone Ivanov remained at the foot of the Cembra pines, picking the seeds out of the cones and relishing their spicy, almost tarry flavour. He then set about skinning the dead squirrels, pausing in this task only to light a small fire and arrange a spit for the roasting of the first carcass. He found the meat stringy and not so flavoursome as the hare's.

His next move was to search for a clearing where he could camp for some days and build up his strength. He found one not far from where he'd killed the squirrels. Much of it was bog, but there was enough grass to attract hares and he laid his snares, more to get the practice of it than the meat. Indeed, he had more meat and Cembra seeds than he could carry, so he decided to enjoy a full ration of both.

He experimented with the Cembra seeds, boiling some in his pannikin, and found he could then pound them into a mash which went down well with the squirrel meat, giving it a savour it lacked. Daily he practised with Rogojin's bow, spending three or four hours at a stretch, aiming at smaller and smaller targets until he was confident he could hit a deer of any size.

When the time came to move on, Ivanov felt not only reinvigorated but more confident. No longer did he peer apprehensively into the forest gloom expecting his pursuers to emerge at any moment. He was sure now they had given up the chase, even the dogged Petrisky. And even if Petrisky did appear, couldn't he, Ivanov, who'd survived so far against all odds, be more than a match for the old man?

Ivanov was gentle by nature, slow to anger, and had never in his life laid his hand violently on another man. But he was tall, big-boned, spare-fleshed – and deceptively strong. He could easily overpower Petrisky, he decided, but he would do it gently. And then he'd turn the old man in the direction he'd come – and give him a few kicks to encourage him on his way.

As he walked Ivanov now gave his mind to the problem

of winter quarters. Back in the camp he and Rogojin had discussed this at length, finally deciding that it was essential to find a cave.

Of course he had his axe and could cut logs to build a cabin, but without nails or any other binding material, how could he possibly seal it against the killing cold of the Arctic winter? There was also the problem of controlling a fire in a wooden hut. He had no metal for a stove, nor had he any tools to trim stone for a chimney.

A cave was the answer. If it were deep enough it would provide a natural insulation against sub-zero temperatures; and if it were high-ceilinged he could build a fire inside and not be choked by the smoke.

With this in mind each morning Ivanov climbed a tree to scan the horizon for any break in the flat monotony of forest. Caves were in rock, he reasoned, and rock was to be found in hillsides, gorges and gullies.

He began to be worried. Would there be no end to the soft-earthed sod he had walked on for so many miles? He hadn't seen any rock or stone, and the countless streams he crossed moved sluggishly in ill-defined, shallow channels which merged into bog without revealing even a pebble.

After he'd stopped to make camp that evening a rumbling in the distance told him that a thunder storm was brewing. He rigged a shelter with spruce branches and decided to sit the storm out before making a fire. He hurriedly collected dried twigs and cones for kindling and covered them with his coat to keep them dry. He then sat huddled in his shelter while the rain bucketed down.

Ever since the cloudburst which had enabled him to escape from Petrisky he had become accustomed to these sudden downpours and now he could tell, by the dropping of the wind and the stillness, when one was due. The storms lasted only minutes, but were hectic, filling the woods with noise which lingered long after the rain had ceased.

But when this storm had passed, Ivanov became suddenly aware of a noise which didn't belong to it. He left his shelter of spruce branches to listen. There it was again, a faint roaring, quite unlike the echo of thunder or the rustling of rain.

'It's a waterfall!' he exclaimed aloud, almost reluctant to believe what his ears told him. How could there conceivably be a waterfall on such flat country?

9

Dusk had already fallen and it was too late to do any exploring that evening, but with first light next morning Ivanov was awake and listening for the sound of the waterfall. It came fainter now, from the south east he judged, and some miles away.

He scrambled up a tree and as he peered through the topmost branches he gasped in surprise at the changed landscape that lay before him. There were no mountains, to be sure, not even a hill, but the monotonous flatness had been broken by a sudden, seemingly precipitous drop in the terrain. It was an escarpment which stretched out of his vision to left and right, and he was looking down on a lower level of flat country disappearing into the blue distance.

He could hardly contain his glee. 'There must be a drop of some two or three hundred feet,' he said to himself wonderingly, 'and there must be a cave somewhere in that tangle of rock.' The escarpment was facing the right way, too, giving shelter from the cold north.

Ivanov was quickly on his way, sometimes breaking into a trot, not bothering now to listen for the waterfall. He couldn't have missed the escarpment if he had tried.

He knew he had reached it when the ground began to fall away from him and the trees became thinner. And then suddenly he was on the brink, out in the sunlight on a boulder-strewn slope of short grass. The drop wasn't precipitous. There were some slides of scree and rock terracing, cliffs some twenty feet high, all falling in a jumble of gentle levels to the forest floor below.

He lay back full length on the turf. It was soft and sprinkled with blue hare-bells. The sun shone hot on his face and from all around him came the tinkling sound of a thousand streamlets carrying the water from the forest above to the forest below. From his left, still muffled by distance, came the roar of the waterfall.

For the first time in years he felt at peace with himself, and for the first time in years he fell asleep – smiling.

When he awoke the sun had passed its zenith. He felt refreshed and decided he would take his time in descending the escarpment so as to get the lay of the land.

He scrambled over some boulders and took a diagonal route towards the sound of the waterfall. As he rounded an outcrop of rock like a miniature tower, a gleam from the forest floor below caught his eye. It was a river, a thin ribbon of water snaking its way in myriad loops, sparkling in the sun like a diamond necklace on green beige.

Ivanov gave a shout of delight. A river meant fish. He must head for it at all costs, he decided, and then realised that the waterfall must be its source.

But as the sound of the fall became louder, so the escarpment became steeper and rockier, and Ivanov decided to head straight down. He was about a hundred feet from the trees below him when the waterfall came into view on his left. It wasn't a fall so much as a series of steeply sloping gullies or chutes, down which the water churned at a furious speed, ending in an immense pool, almost a lake, with shingle shores.

The trees began some distance from the lake, and in between lay stretches of grass growing between shelves of rock and shingle. The air was still and warmer than Ivanov had ever experienced since arriving in the Far North. That was because of the shelter given by the escarpment, he decided.

He stopped on the shingle beside the little lake and felt himself enclosed in a cosy oasis, freed from the gloom of the forest. He screwed up his eyes against the evening sun and took in the scene of rock and grass and water. He breathed deeply. This was it – this was his winter home!

He camped that night on a grassy shelf between the cliff and the lake, and next morning began his search for a cave, starting with the rocky outcrop at the base of the escarpment. He scrambled up the cliff, crossing the conduits and walking so far that the noise of the rushing waters became faint. But he found nothing, not even a hollow or cavity of any sort which could have been walled up with rocks or timber on its open end.

Disheartened, he returned to the lake, wondering if after all he couldn't build a cabin of logs sound enough to resist the Arctic winter. He could use turf to pack the roof and the gaps between the logs. Wouldn't it be snugger than a cave?

It sounded feasible, but how was he to fashion the timber with his primitive axe? Finding trees of matching girth and felling them would be a big enough task. To get them to fit together snugly and securely was beyond him. Hammer and nails, saw and chisel were what he needed. And even then he doubted his skill. A garden shed was more in his line, he reflected ruefully. How willingly he'd exchange now his hard-won degrees for a course in basic carpentry!

A movement which caught the corner of his eye

brought his thoughts to an abrupt halt. He had been looking across the lake and whatever had moved was on his left, in the tangle of rocks which lay between the lake and the escarpment.

He scanned the base of the cliffs but could see nothing; then he realised with a shock he'd been looking too far. Between him and the cliffs, only a hundred yards away, its form melting into the background of russet rocks, was a bear.

10

Back in the camp Rogojin had told him: 'Watch out for bears. They won't bother you normally, but in the mating season the males sometimes go berserk and will attack anything on sight. And steer clear of a mother bear with cubs. She can be nasty. Otherwise there's nothing to worry about.'

Sound advice, Ivanov didn't doubt, but not exactly comforting with a bear almost within spitting distance. It was a huge specimen, more than five feet from nose to tail. Was it male or female? Did it have cubs?

The bear was watching him intently, and as Ivanov fumbled for his axe-shaft, it reared itself on two legs and gave a brief roar, rather like the bark of a giant dog.

Ivanov backed away. Rogojin had warned him not to appear to challenge a bear. 'If you do the retreating he won't follow you.'

To Ivanov's immense relief, Rogojin was proved right. After another abrupt roar, the bear shambled off on all fours and had soon crossed the boulder-strewn stretch of grass and shingle to disappear into the woods.

Bears use caves to hibernate in during the winter, mused Ivanov. Could the bear have come from a cave it was now abandoning for the summer? He thought he'd already searched the base of the cliffs, but there were so many large boulders he might easily have overlooked an opening.

He was about four feet up the cliff, on a narrow ledge, when a pungent animal smell, rather like a wet dog, led him to a slight overhang. Immediately beneath it was a narrow, slit-like opening, about six feet long and three feet high.

Ivanov viewed it cautiously. It seemed ideal for his purposes; in fact, it couldn't be better, tucked away as it was beneath the overhang of rock, which served as a natural porch. But was it occupied?

Bracing himself for immediate flight, Ivanov tossed a fist-sized rock through the opening. He heard it clatter inside and then land with a dull thud on something soft. Litter left by the bears, he reasoned. He'd have some clearing out to do before making this cave his home.

He threw in another rock to make doubly sure. There was no roar, no grunt, no sound of movement of any sort. Levering himself up on his elbows he peered through the opening.

After the bright sunlight Ivanov could see nothing to begin with, but as his eyes became accustomed to the gloom he found himself looking into a roughly rounded chamber, about twelve feet across and eight feet high. The floor of the chamber was about four feet below the opening, which served as a window.

Ivanov hitched a leg over the edge of the opening and was about to drop inside when his foot touched something soft and yielding. He gasped and looked down. Lying full-length on the floor, close against the rock wall immediately below the opening, was a bear.

29

In one continuous movement Ivanov vaulted through the opening, landing on his feet outside the cave. Seconds later he was at the lake, looking fearfully back.

But quick as Ivanov had moved, his reasoning moved quicker. Even as he fled he realised no bear would wait for somebody to step on it. The creature must be sick or dead.

He returned to the foot of the cliff and from there tossed stones through the slit above him. All was quiet. He clambered onto the ledge and took another look through the opening. It was a bear all right, and it was certainly dead. He poked at it with his axe-shaft and it didn't stir.

It took Ivanov the rest of that day to haul the dead bear from the cave. He had to cut logs to act as a ramp to slide the animal up the four feet to the opening. It was too heavy to lift.

How long the bear had been dead Ivanov couldn't tell, but the carcass had not yet begun to smell and the fur was in good condition. He skinned it as best he could with his old bread knife, hacking away with the axe at difficult spots.

It was a she bear and why it had died mystified him until he found a puncture in the hide slightly below the heart. He gouged the flesh out with his knife and found a bullet embedded in the lung. As he removed it a fountain of blood squirted over his hands. Obviously the poor creature had bled internally.

The bullet worried Ivanov. Out there in the middle of the taiga, hundreds of miles from any prison camp or settlement, there were no casual hunters. It must have been Petrisky who shot the bear. But when and where? It could have happened a week ago and the bear could have travelled miles before retreating to the cave to die.

And Ivanov understood now the presence of the other bear. 'They are solitary creatures,' Rogojin had told him, 'and get together only for the mating season.' Probably the bear he'd seen was a male which had been courting the dying female.

I I

Having pegged out the bear's skin to dry, Ivanov dragged the carcass the length of the lake and pushed it into a conduit at the outlet. The rushing waters swept it out of sight. To have meat like that lying around rotting in the sun would have attracted wolves.

'Keep a clean camp,' Rogojin had told him, 'otherwise you'll have a wolf or two haunting the place, waiting for scraps like jackals.'

This had surprised Ivanov. His idea of the wolf was the rapacious hunter of his boyhood books, scouring the taiga for prey and treeing hapless trappers and other humans who dared cross its path.

'It's true they're cunning hunters,' Rogojin had conceded, 'but if you're going to save them the bother of hunting by cluttering your camp with carrion they'll hang around for days, frightening away all the game you're hoping to hunt for yourself. They can be a real nuisance.'

'And dangerous too, I suppose,' Ivanov had suggested.

'Not at all,' was Rogojin's surprising answer. 'Wolves have never been known to attack a man, not even when they're starving. All those exciting tales of narrow escapes from ravenous packs are just tales – part of our folklore.'

At the time Ivanov hadn't known whether to be believed or disappointed, but now he felt that no matter how wolves reacted to man he could well do without having them prowling round his cave. He made quite sure that the bear's carcass was washed down the conduit and out into the river below.

He then cleaned out the cave carefully, scraping up all the litter left by the bears and covering the floor with a thick layer of sand and gravel from the lake. This he had to carry laboriously in his satchel and he decided that one of his first tasks once he had settled down was to make a bucket, or container of some sort.

His next concern was to seal the opening to the cave so as to make it weatherproof for the winter. And he would have to devise something strong enough to discourage bears or any other animals from trying to make a home of the cave again.

Ivanov's first idea was a barrier of logs which he would drive into the ground below the cave. But as the cave was some eight feet up the side of a rocky terrace or little cliff in the escarpment he would need logs fifteen feet high or more in order to cover the opening.

Such a barrier would stand out against the rockface – an obvious human artefact, advertising his presence. And while Ivanov realised that the chances of anyone, apart from Petrisky, wandering into his corner of the taiga were remote in the extreme, he didn't want to invite company – human or animal.

Then he noticed that about four feet below the cave there was a narrow ledge, only inches wide in parts but running horizontally for the entire breadth of the opening. If he could cut logs to fit they could then be wedged upright between the ledge and the overhang of rock above the cave.

It wasn't easy to find trees to give him logs of the right girth, but Ivanov decided this was such an important task he should not hurry it. Repeatedly he had to sharpen his axe, the metal losing its edge too quickly for his comfort. At this rate, and using rough rock for sharpening, the axe-head would swiftly wear away.

He tried to chop out a flat surface on one side of each of the logs so that they would fit together snugly. He ruined three logs before he got the knack of it and even then the flattened surface was rough and irregular. He would ram turf into the crevices between the logs, he decided.

Fitting the logs between the ledge and the overhang proved much easier than he'd dared hope. By hammering in flat stones beneath each log he found he could wedge the logs in so tightly that even the strongest bear would have found it difficult to prise them out. He left a narrow opening at one end to act as a doorway, which would be plugged from inside by two shorter logs to be jammed between the sill of the opening and the overhang.

When he had finished, Ivanov clambered into the cave and fixed his 'door' behind him. Though quite a high wind was blowing outside, hardly a draught penetrated the timbering. It was certainly snow-proof, he decided, but he'd make doubly sure of that by plugging the crevices with turf from the inside as well as the outside.

Using boulders he carried in from the base of the cliff, he arranged a neat little fireplace near the 'doorway' and started a small blaze with pine cones, feeding it carefully with faggots chopped from the limbs of a dead tree. The dry wood burnt steadily, making little smoke but giving off enough heat to take the chill out of the cave.

Ivanov surveyed his new home and nodded approvingly. It would make a snug retreat. He'd put the bearskin on the floor in front of the fire and make his bed of birch leaves on it. There he'd be safe from the killing cold of deepest winter – even cosy. He smiled happily. Rogojin had insisted that the key to survival in the taiga was an adequate winter refuge. This he had found.

Part Two

WINTER QUARTERS

12

Having solved the problem of shelter Ivanov's next con
cern was food – not only for his immediate needs but fo
the winter as well. Rogojin had warned him that as th
summer waned and the days closed in he'd find it in
creasingly difficult to track down game. He must hunt nov
for the lean days that lay ahead and learn how to preserv
the meat by drying it in the sun. When the time was righ
he'd look out for cranberries and bilberries and dry thes
too. Together with Cembra seed and any other nuts h
chanced upon, they would constitute a valuable hardtacl
reserve.

But first he wanted to try his hand at fishing. His tackl
was a length of twine and a half dozen hooks made fron
the barbs of barbed wire. Rogojin's handiwork again
He'd taken the wire from a perimeter fence right unde
the nose of a guard.

Ivanov made for the conduit at the outlet of the lak
and followed it down for a mile or more until the land flat
tened out and the rushing waters eased into a narrow
slow-flowing stream. Rivulets from the escarpment joine
the stream on both sides and soon it grew into a sizeabl
river, shallow but twenty feet wide in parts.

The forest had again closed in and Ivanov found i
easier going to wade through the water. When he reache

pool he made for the bank and cast his first line, using as bait grubs he found under the bark of a dead pine.

It seemed ages before he felt a tugging on the line, and when he withdrew it he found the maggot gone. He bent the hook inwards and tried again. This time the twine was almost pulled out of his hand, and he landed a fish about nine inches long, a trout he guessed it to be.

Ivanov knew nothing about fishing, but as he landed one fish after the other until he had six squirming on the bank beside him, he realised he was astonishingly lucky. It must be the bait, he decided, and examined his maggots carefully to make sure he'd remember the type.

How long he would have remained on the bank, the sun warm on his back, the only sound the tinkling of the little river, he didn't know. But a cawing of crows in the distance made him look up.

They were flying in a tight circle above the forest about half a mile away. As he watched they were joined by others. 'Carrion,' he thought. 'There might be something there I can skin.'

He packed the fish into his satchel, which he secured by its strap to the branches of a larch, safe from any furry marauders. He'd pick the catch up on his way back.

Following the crows' raucous cries he swiftly arrived at the spot where they were wheeling overhead and sank to the ground to make a cautious survey on all fours. He didn't want to walk into a wounded bear or a dying wolverine.

And so it was, on his hands and knees, that he discovered what was left of poor Petrisky.

The old man was lying on his back. A gaping wound stretched diagonally across his body, from heart to groin, and his intestines had spilled onto the ground beside him. The crows had already pecked out the eyes, which gave the face a glaring look.

Ivanov shuddered. This was the work of the dead bear.

35

Petrisky had shot her but that one bullet, though fatal in the end, hadn't checked the violence of her charge. I must have been a fearsome struggle.

Still grasped in Petrisky's left hand was his hunting knife, long, slightly curved and razor sharp. Even after the bear had closed with him he'd managed at least to draw the knife, if not to use it.

Gently Ivanov prised the fingers loose. It wasn't difficult. Rigor mortis had long passed and the body was already smelling badly. He held his breath as he pocketed the hunting knife. Where was Petrisky's rifle?

He found it in the branches of a nearby spruce, flung there by the enraged bear. The wooden stock was shattered into splinters and the barrel was bent back on itself, unusable, beyond repair. Ivanov sighed. That rifle could have solved his food problem.

He returned to the body. His first impulse was to bury Petrisky as he was, but he realised he needed everything the old man had on him, not only the haversack still strapped to his back, but his clothes and boots, even his underwear and socks.

Twice Ivanov had to stop to retch, leaning miserably against a tree trunk, his back to the corpse. He hadn't even seen a dead man before. Now he had the task of stripping one, with the flesh already putrid.

When he'd finished he dug a shallow grave with his axe and covered the naked corpse as best he could with earth and debris from the forest floor, finally felling a small tree to lay across the mound. He felt that should discourage any scavengers.

The old man had been wearing a fur-lined jacket when he met the bear, and it must have been unbuttoned at the time, for it was untorn and only slightly bloodstained. Ivanov felt its warm thickness and realised how threadbare his own prison-issue clothing had become. But it was the haversack which gave him most delight.

It contained a blanket, a sleeping bag, spare trousers and shirt, a repair kit with needles, cotton and a ball of yarn, a small cauldron with a handle for hanging over a fire, two spoons, a tin plate and a tin mug, a hatchet and a coil of stout rope.

In a side pocket of the haversack were two boxes of matches, one almost empty, and a brass tinder box complete with flint-and-wheel and tapers soaked in paraffin wax.

It was the tinder box he treasured most. Striking a spark with Rogojin's flint and broken file and trying to ignite dried fir needles from it, had been despairingly laborious. Now he could light a fire in style!

Ivanov used the rope to tie the old man's possessions into a neat bundle, but before setting off for the cave he paused at the grave.

Knowing that Petrisky was on his trail had been a worry, he admitted to himself, but in a way it had been comforting to know another man might be somewhere near in this endless wilderness.

Now he knew there was no one. He was truly alone in the taiga.

'Goodbye, Petrisky,' he muttered. 'And good hunting.'

13

The short summer flew by. Ivanov was out each day with bow and arrows, snares and fishing tackle. The trout from the river were his easiest catch, but his experiments in trying to preserve the fish for his winter larder were a disaster. Neither drying in the sun nor smoking over a fire of dampened fir needles checked corruption. He had a bad bout of vomiting and diarrhoea after testing some of this noisome tack.

He was more successful with meat, carefully following a method Rogojin had described in detail. First he dried strips of lean meat in the sun, having scraped off all the fat. He then pounded the meat into shreds, using a hollow boulder as a mortar and a smooth piece of rock as pestle. The fat he boiled down in Petrisky's cauldron and while it was still liquid mixed it with the shredded lean. As the fat coagulated he pressed the mixture into balls, which reminded him of the meat dumplings or faggots his mother had been so fond of making.

Rogojin had assured him that so long as he kept the faggots dry they would remain edible for months. He also suggested that in late summer, when bilberries could be found, these should be pounded and mixed in with the fat to give the faggots flavour. Ivanov did this and was agreeably surprised to find how palatable they became, the bilberries in some way making up for the salt which he so sorely missed.

His stock of meat came from hare, squirrel and suslik. The latter he found in burrows which honeycombed grassy areas of the escarpment. They were fat with their summer feeding, fully primed for the long hibernation which lay ahead. These ground squirrels were tastier than the tree squirrels, but were so small that after converting the meat into faggots a half dozen hardly made a meal.

Of deer he saw not a sign, though he wandered far from the cave, Rogojin's bow at the ready. He was expert in the use of this weapon now, and he had the chance of testing its accuracy when he found a wolverine devouring a hare caught in one of his snares.

The glutton was about four feet long, thickly built like a young bear. Seeing Ivanov it dropped its prey and eyed him speculatively, seemingly quite unafraid.

For a moment Ivanov wondered if he shouldn't retreat. Rogojin had told him that wolverines were ferocious and cunning, able to take on creatures twice their size. But he stood firm. It was time he proved to himself that he was really a hunter, and in any case he wanted the glutton's fur. He guessed rightly that the meat of such an indiscriminate carnivore would be uneatable.

He dropped to one knee and took careful aim at the wolverine's throat. The arrow flew true, burying itself deep under the snapping jaws. Screaming with pain and fury and clawing at the arrow shaft, the wolverine made for the trees. Ivanov followed, Petrisky's hatchet in one hand and his hunting knife in the other. But there was no need for a coup de grace. The arrow must have pierced the jugular and he found the wolverine bleeding to death, eyes already glazed, but teeth bared and snarling with its very last breath.

Squirrels proved an easy target. Their favourite trees were pine, and Ivanov would stand under the trees, perfectly still, and wait. He had his bow trained on a squirrel one morning when a slight movement on the bough below his quarry caught his eye. He let fly and a sable fell at his feet. It had silver-tipped, blue-black fur, soft as down.

Ivanov took great care in skinning the sable, marvelling that such a slim, elegant little predator should belong to the same weasel family as the ungainly glutton. He decided to make a muffler with the fur. The meat was inedible.

As the days grew shorter and each morning brought a heavier frost, heralding the swift approach of winter, Ivanov realised he had to choose between wandering further afield in search of deer or concentrating on building up a store of squirrel meat. He hadn't the time for both.

While fishing that morning he'd noticed ice on the water. Very soon his fish would be moving downstream, well beyond a day's trek, and very soon too the sun would lose its warmth, making it impossible for him to dry out meat for his faggots.

Separating the lean meat from the fat in such small carcasses as hare, squirrel and suslik was a desperately slow process, and when Ivanov calculated how much of this meat he must preserve to last out the winter he was horrified. The simple arithmetic of it made survival plainly impossible.

At all costs he had to find bigger game – roebuck or elk – so that he could set to work preserving sizeable portions of meat in the little time left to him.

He began to wonder if his part of the taiga was too dense for deer. There were few clearings, and the only extensive stretches of grass were on the scree-strewn terraces of the escarpment. Yet Rogojin had assured him that roebuck wandered far north in the summer, travelling miles from the deciduous woods in the south to search out the sweet grass of the taiga clearings. While elk, Rogojin had insisted, could be found in the taiga the year round. Their favourite diet was the shoots and twigs of deciduous saplings, especially willow, which thrived in the marshy tracts.

Ivanov didn't doubt this was true, but neither could he deny he had seen not a single sign of any deer within striking distance of his cave. He'd have to hunt further afield; a trek south for thirty miles or more might prove fruitful.

14

Before leaving he blocked the 'door' to his cave with heavy logs which he jammed under the overhang, and having packed Petrisky's haversack with all that he might need on a lengthy trip, he made for the river.

It would have doubled his journey to follow the course

of the river through all its wild loops and curves, but he
kept it within easy reach, not only for the fishing, but
because the water might attract game.

After three days of steady plodding without seeing a
sign of a deer, Ivanov decided to head due west into the
taiga in the hope of striking grassy clearings. He had
enough suslik faggots, supplemented by fish he'd caught
that morning, to keep him going for fifty miles or more.

He'd left the river far behind when he made camp that
night, and as he prepared a fire to broil his fish, he found he
missed the sound of running water. It had been a
reassuringly homely noise, reminding him of summer
bivouacs beside a gentle tributary of the Don.

Each summer they'd gone to the same spot and camped
the night, his whole family – father, mother, two brothers
and three sisters. And it was on one of these trips that
he'd first met Katerina.

He'd been at the water's edge washing the supper
dishes with his mother when out of the twilight came the
slim figure of a young girl, paddling her way through the
shallows beside the bank.

'Watch out for deep pools,' he'd called. 'They can give
you a sudden ducking.'

She'd approached them, one hand holding the skirt of
her cotton dress clear of the water, the other clutching a
pair of sandals. She had a freckled, sunburnt face and
cool, grey eyes.

'Stop it!' Ivanov suddenly shouted to himself, kicking
savagely at the fire and sending skewered pieces of fish
sizzling among the trees.

He crouched over the embers, arms folded tight round
his body, hugging himself for comfort as he tried to keep
at bay the black despair which threatened to engulf him.
He must not, he resolved, think of Katerina, at least not
now, not when thoughts of the past could sap his will to
survive. To daydream was to die.

He scraped together the dying fire, blew it into flames, then searched patiently for his pieces of skewered fish. As he replaced them on the spit the night air seemed heavy with the smell of smoke. 'What a mess I've made,' he murmured to himself, stamping on the ashes scattered by his kick.

Next morning Ivanov awoke well before dawn to find himself coughing and spluttering in a thin veil of smoke. He leapt to his feet, cursing himself for that intemperate kick at the fire the night before. But his fire was out, the ashes cold to the touch.

Slowly he straightened himself, struggling to contain the panic which he felt welling from the pit of his stomach. This was no bonfire. That smell of smoke the night before hadn't been from the scattered ashes of his own little fire.

The smoke was coming from the west, driven on a brisk breeze, and he turned sideways to it to listen. 'It'll be like thunder,' Rogojin had told him. 'Like no noise you've ever heard.'

It was more like a continuous roll of explosions, more like those massive artillery barrages Ivanov had read about.

He scrambled up a spruce and gasped at what he saw. The western skyline, in a wide arc from north to south, was hidden under a thick bank of smoke which glowed a fiery red, fanned by the wind into a pulsating furnace which was sweeping towards him at an alarming pace.

With frantic speed he packed his haversack and set off east at a steady lope, his one thought to reach the river, some twelve miles away. Narrow as it was, the river provided the only break in the forest which might serve as a barrier to the flames.

Ivanov maintained a breath-rasping pace, stopping only to listen for the thunder of the fire behind him. He had no time now to climb a tree to look back: the wind had risen and streamers of smoke eddying past convinced him he was losing ground.

He was now conscious, for the first time since being in the taiga, of animal life around him. He saw nothing at first, only heard the creak and rustle of creatures making their way, like him, at speed through the woods. But as the smoke increased and the roaring of the fire cut out all the other sounds, he caught a glimpse of a bear ahead of him.

He thought to change direction slightly, but at that moment a lynx bounded across his path, its teeth bared in a fixed snarl of fear. It didn't give him so much as a passing glance, and he realised he need not worry about the bear. No animal had a mind for anything but escape from the awesome fury of the fire.

He was running now, weaving in and out of the trees, taking direction from the moving canopy of smoke which blotted out the sky above him. He tried to avoid thickets and overgrown clearings, but again and again he stumbled into them and found himself scrambling over toppled tree trunks and through tangled copses of young birch.

His breath was coming in shuddering gasps and he had little control over his legs, which felt heavy as lead, calf and thigh muscles twitching spasmodically. The fire could now be felt in the wind, like a hot blanket on his back, and he was bathed in sweat, which filled his eyes and blurred his vision.

He tried to leap over a fallen tree, but his legs buckled under him, and as he fell to the ground he took in a lungful of smoke which doubled him up in a paroxysm of coughing. He struggled to his feet to avoid the smoke swirling at knee level and fought to control his coughing, gulping for air with the strident rasping of a drowning man.

As soon as he could breath again he wiped the sweat from his face with his sleeve and looked round him. The woods had been darkened by the pall of smoke overhead, but he could see clearly enough to observe how the smoke at knee level moved in scattered spurts, spreading upwards to meet the smoke overhead. In between were pockets clear of smoke.

Telling himself to stop charging through the woods like a panicking bear, Ivanov walked swiftly from one clear patch to another, muffling his face with his sleeve where the smoke rose above his head. At first he made steady progress due east, but then he found that in following the smokeless pockets he was travelling almost parallel with the fire.

Fighting an impulse to run, he stopped and faced east – towards the river. A warm current of air swirled past him, and for a joyous moment he thought the wind had swung round, was now blowing against the fire. But then the horrifying truth made him stagger forward in a lurching trot. He was in the fire draught, on the edge of the dread hurricane which sucked all before it into the maw of the furnace.

The thunder of the blaze seemed all round him now, and the forest was bathed in an eerie red light, yet he saw no flames. The hot breeze blowing against him became a wind, bending the trees, searing his lungs. He knew he had only moments now before his agony was ended, and he determined to keep moving, to die on his feet.

Suddenly he was falling, tumbling head over heels down a steep bank to find himself sitting in water. 'The river!' he shouted, but the sound emerged as a croak from his scorched lips. On his hands and knees he shuffled through the water, searching for a deep pool.

At that point the river had made one of its loop-like curves, splitting into two channels with a strip of sand and pebbles in between. In the channel running against the east bank Ivanov found a pool which was shoulder deep.

He gasped as the icy water closed about him. A moment ago he was being scorched and now he was being frozen.

But the wild scene unfolding before him took all thoughts from his own condition. The blanket of smoke flying high on the westerly wind had deepened to blot out all light from the sun, and the ghostly red twilight he'd noticed in the woods was spreading over the river.

The roaring of the still unseen flames mingled with the howling winds of the firestorm to become a high pitched screech, a mad keening which made Ivanov cringe in his pool, horrified by its sheer savagery.

The trees on the west bank bent to the blast of the firestorm and then exploded into flames from top to bottom. They didn't burn as Ivanov imagined they would. With resin oozing out of them, and already dried to tinder by the firewind, the trees just disintegrated – reduced to carbon in one explosive puff.

Some instinct made him snatch a deep breath and duck his head. As he did so he felt the water rise, as though sucked up by the vacuum created by the fire, and warm currents welled up from the river bed. For an awful moment he thought the water was beginning to boil.

Lungs bursting, Ivanov cautiously raised his head to find the air still hot and thick with smoke which swirled over the river from the blackened wilderness on the west bank.

He turned to the east and staggered back, awestruck. The fire had leapt the river and now he was seeing it from behind, a wall of flame towering a hundred feet above the taiga, twisting and dipping, swaying and curling in a ballet of destruction.

Ivanov dragged himself wearily from the water onto the strip of sand between the channels. The air was still warm, but breathable now, and the smoke was thinning fast. The sun broke through and glistened on something wet and brown lying half out of the water. He leant forward,

peering uncertainly, his eyes smarting from the smoke. It
was an elk, a full grown bull, its lungs burnt out in the hot
blast when the firestorm leapt the river.

The elk moved feebly and Ivanov despatched it with
one slash of Petrisky's hunting knife across the jugular.
As he watched it bleed, holding the antlered head to keep
the gash in its throat open, he shook his head in bemused
wonderment. That forest fire, which had so nearly cost
him his life, had given him what he came so far for: a deer.

15

It would have been an impossible task to haul the elk all
the way back to the cave, and in any case, by the time he
got there the late summer sun would have become too
weak to dry out the meat for making winter faggots. So
Ivanov decided to make camp on the sandbank and deal
with the elk on the spot.

To reduce such a large carcass to balls of shredded
meat and boiled fat was a long and tedious task, but he
accepted it happily, knowing that the reward of his labour
was a well-stocked larder which would take him through
the first months of winter, and possibly for longer.

He made so many faggots that he was hard put to find a
way of carrying them. He wrapped the fragile balls of
meat in the hide of the elk, using grass for packing, but
then found the load too heavy to hoist onto his shoulders.
A sledge would have been the answer, but building one
was beyond his skill.

Finally he settled for a drag pole, cutting down a five-
foot birch sapling to which he tied the load securely. Then
with thongs of deerskin he made a crude shoulder harness
which he fastened to the thick end of the pole. Hitching

himself into the harness he found he could drag the pole along smoothly and with a minimum of strain.

Progress was slow. Where possible he kept to the side of the river, for he found it difficult to make an easy way through the black confusion of burnt tree stumps and branches left by the forest fire. There was hardly a tree standing for as many miles as he could see, and the few that were still upright only added to the desolation by their gaunt, scorched outline.

It was while searching for serviceable remnants of timber for his camp fire one evening that Ivanov made a discovery which was to prove a boon in the winter months ahead.

Scuffling with his foot in the ashes he turned up a four-foot length of root which was pure charcoal. He was quick to realise this was the best possible fuel for burning in his cave, for not only was it smokeless, but it was long lasting and gave off a more radiant heat than wood. It needed a constant draught to burn effectively, but he could solve that problem at his leisure. In fact, once winter closed in he'd have all the time in the world to fan the charcoal by hand if needs be. In any case he'd be using chopped wood as well for fuel. The charcoal would be a stand-by for the coldest months.

A more careful search among the ashes revealed that much of the timber growing at ground level and buried in the thick, airless carpet of needles on the forest floor, had been roasted by the fire into charcoal.

What a pity he was so far from the cave, was his first thought, but then it occurred to him there was no need to return to this burnt wilderness for a supply of the precious fuel. Nearer home, in fact within a few miles of his cave, were burnt tracts of forest, now overgrown by scrub admittedly, but doubtless with charcoal intact in the topsoil, ready for the taking.

Greatly encouraged by this discovery Ivanov hastened

his steady plodding, thinking now of his cave as a cosy refuge. The days had drawn in and the nights were becoming bitterly cold, and when at last he left the burnt forest and found himself in green woods again, his immense relief was tempered by a cold blast from the north which carried the smell of snow in it.

It took him two more days to reach the cave, battling his way for the last three hours through a blizzard which threatened at times to bring him to a complete halt, such was the force of the wind. But he was not unduly worried. It was too early for the buran to blow – the Siberian blizzard of midwinter which can kill a man, literally freeze him in his tracks.

Yet, this first snow was a timely warning of the rigours that lay ahead and Ivanov knew that he must give priority now to making his cave as warm as possible.

His first concern was to collect charcoal before the ground froze. As he'd guessed, there was an abundance of it in the scrub-covered clearings near the cave, and though much of the charcoal had crumbled to enrich the thin tilth, he dug up enough to make a large stack at the back of his cave. There it would be ready to hand, and should a buran begin to blow he wouldn't have to leave the cave for fuel.

But the charcoal was intended to supplement the logs he'd be using chiefly for the fire, so he built an immense pile of dead timber in a cleft in the cliff, near enough to the cave for convenience, but out of sight should – though it was inconceivable – anyone come that way.

His next task was to re-seal the gaps between the logs which covered the cave opening. The turf he'd used in the Spring had dried out and become too crumbly to be weatherproof. He found that on the terraces of the escarpment the turf under the snow was still soft and he dug it up easily. As he plugged the cracks between the logs the turf froze hard, making as firm a sealing as cement. He couldn't have chosen a better time to do the job.

The hide of the elk he'd killed on the river hadn't had time to dry out so he fastened it to the inside of the logs like a curtain, jamming it into position with wooden wedges. There it would not only help keep out the draught but would dry gradually without going mouldy.

While fixing this 'curtain' he put his mind to the problem of providing a flue for the fire. The more effectively he excluded wind and draught, the more difficult it would be to get his fire to burn efficiently, particularly when he wanted to use the charcoal.

What he needed was a length of pipe which could be thrust through the barricade of logs to bring a draught bearing directly on the fire. The hollowed out limb of a tree might serve the purpose, but he despaired of finding a piece of wood that had rotted so conveniently, with the outside of it still sound and usable. And to hollow out a log with his knife would have taken the whole winter.

It was then that he thought of Petrisky's rifle which the bear had wrecked, shattering the stock and twisting the barrel so that it could never be fired again. That bent barrel was the answer.

Using two boulders on the lakeside for leverage, Ivanov managed to straighten it. He then made a funnel from a piece of elkskin, using a length of his precious snare wire as a framework. He fastened the funnel to one end of the barrel and pushed the other end through a crack between the logs covering the cave opening, sealing it firmly into position with turf. He made a hole in his 'curtain' of elkskin, and about eight inches of the barrel then protruded into the cave, the end resting on the boulders which served as his fireplace.

He was delighted to find that the wind, caught by the funnel, whistled through the barrel. To cut out the draught when it was not needed he whittled a small wooden plug, wrapping it in deerskin.

Anxious now to test his flue, he entered the cave, wedging the doorway logs securely behind him and covering them with a corner of the elkhide he'd cut specially for this purpose. He made a small fire of wood and placed on it some pieces of charcoal. As the wood burnt away he unplugged the flue and the draught from the barrel played on the charcoal, which burst into flame, almost white-hot and smokeless.

Ivanov sat back on his haunches, his customarily tense features relaxing into a boyish grin as the heat from the little fire filled the cave and the light from it bathed the grim rock walls in a warm glow. What he'd made in effect was a miniature forge which would heat up the cave and cook his food in half the time taken by a wood fire.

A bed was his next concern. During the summer he'd been content to sleep on a pile of dried birch leaves, using Petrisky's sleeping bag when the nights were chill. It was an untidy bed, the leaves spreading over the floor of the cave and blowing about in the slightest draught.

He still intended to use the leaves, for they insulated the cold from the stone floor and were soft and yielding – in fact, a perfect mattress. But he'd box them in, he decided.

He'd already cut and shaped the wood in the summer, and using strips of birch bark as cord he fashioned a framework of logs, about 18 inches high, two feet wide and six feet long. He filled this with the birch leaves, pressing them down hard, but leaving a space of some four inches between the top layer and the top of the box.

Then using Petrisky's needle and thread he made a pillow out of the sable skin which he'd originally intended to use as a muffler. With the silky blue-black fur on the outside and stuffed with dried moss it made a luxurious cushion, giving his crude bed an almost sybaritic touch.

Laying Petrisky's sleeping bag on the leaves he climbed into the box and stretched out, his head on the sable pillow. The leaves sank slightly so that he was enclosed within the top logs of the framework, as if he were in a ship's bunk.

'It's a free-standing bunk – another Ivanov invention,' he announced aloud with mock pride. 'But it could be a bloody coffin, too,' he added wryly.

He positioned the bunk four feet from the fire and in between laid the skin of the bear he had found dead in the cave. The hide had dried out perfectly, but was as stiff as a board.

The wolverine skin he'd treated with more care, kneading it daily as it dried, rolling and unrolling it so that now it was soft and pliable. Rogojin had told him that of all furs the wolverine's was the most highly prized for its warmth and its capacity to resist water. He intended making a waistcoat of it, for wearing outside Petrisky's fur-lined jacket.

16

That night a buran set in. There wasn't much snow but the wind from the north was a marrow chiller, so intensely cold that Ivanov dared not venture outside for three days.

He occupied his time chipping away at a log which he was making into a bucket. It was a painfully slow task, for he had to use his old bread knife in lieu of a chisel. He could have made a quicker job of it with Petrisky's hunting knife, but he dared not risk snapping the slender blade.

As he worked he took stock of his condition. He was always hungry – that was to be expected – but he felt fit and had rid himself of the crippling lethargy which had afflicted him in the prison camp. He put that down to the protein he was now getting; just one of his faggots was worth twenty bowls of the prison skilly.

He was also free of the boils which had bothered him in the camp, and he noticed that now, when he cut himself or scraped a knee, the wound healed quickly without festering.

This was because in the summer he'd searched the clearings for edible plants, tasting all that he'd found. Some were too bitter and others too coarse to chew; one raised painful blisters on his tongue and lips.

Undeterred, he carried on with his experiments until he discovered, almost hidden in the grass, a completely prostrate little plant with leaves like a dandelion. It had a refreshing bitter-sweet flavour and was crisp to the tooth, making it easy to chew and swallow. He tried boiling it, but it then became slimy and tasteless, so he decided to use it as a salad.

As soon as berries appeared on the shrubby growth in the clearings he ate them indiscriminately to begin with, and then learnt to recognise the sweeter ones. These, boiled with the fresh meat of hare, made a tasty stew.

He tried drying the berries in the sun so as to preserve them for the winter, but they either went mouldy or shrivelled up into fleshless fragments of seed and skin. This was the one tip Rogojin had given him which didn't work.

Now, with the onset of winter, he was of course deprived of both his 'greens' and his berries, but he hoped he'd built up a sufficient reserve of vitamins in his body to balance the all-meat diet which lay ahead.

Loneliness would now trouble him, he realised, for in the summer he'd been too busy hunting, fishing and making his faggots to miss the companionship of the prison camp. Being cooped up in the cave for days on end or perhaps weeks when the buran blew would be a new ordeal.

And yet, when he thought back to life in the camp he found that what he then missed most of all he still missed, and that was books. He would have rejoiced to have

Rogojin share his cave, for he had a deep and enduring affection for the man, but if he had to choose between a book and anyone else from the camp, he would have chosen the book.

Ivanov felt vaguely uneasy about this, as though he were guilty of a betrayal, but he argued to himself that from boyhood on he had become so accustomed to using his mind that it was perfectly natural for him to feel the need for mental exercise, for a purely abstract challenge which had nothing to do with the physical problems besetting him. He couldn't deny his hunger for the printed word, a hunger as real as that for food.

But in any case, he told himself, he'd have plenty to think about, for now that the immediate challenge of keeping alive had been met thanks to his reserve of faggots, he could relax and daydream as much as he liked about home.

He would imagine walking in on Katerina and little Alyosha, see in their faces the surprised delight, the love. It would be a sunny summer's morning, he decided, and Alyosha would be playing trains in the dust of the yard. Through the window he'd see Katerina in the kitchen, head bent on a homely chore, sweeping back with her forearm that stray lock of hair.

And by some miracle he'd be a free man again, not a runaway prisoner. He'd return to his college, smile into the bright faces of his students and take up the broken threads of the labour he so loved.

It was thoughts such as these which sustained Ivanov in the first months of the long winter. He was out all day with his bow, searching in the snow for the track of elk or checking and re-setting the snares he'd laid for hares.

But he didn't wander far, for always in his mind was the prospect of the evening to come, crouched over his charcoal fire, seeing faces in the flames and figures dancing in the shadows of the cave....

17

One of the faces he often imagined seeing was Leykin's. It was a homely face, low-browed and bulbous-nosed, quite unlike what Ivanov expected in a poet. But the eyes were compelling, a luminous brown and always wide open – not staring – but widened as if in wonder at what they saw.

Leykin had turned up from nowhere to teach English at Ivanov's college and his appointment had aroused a buzz of speculation. Not even the principal had been consulted. Then the word went round: he'd been a *zek*, a political prisoner.

Those were the heady days of 'de-Stalinisation' when bolder spirits at the college openly criticised Stalin's rule and even dared suggest that instead of being the 'little father' of his people the dead dictator had been a megalomanic tyrant. There were no reprisals, for the local *apparatchiks* – the party bosses – were bewildered to find that their new leaders were themselves calling Stalin worse names than that.

This opened the floodgates of abuse and not unnaturally it was thought that Leykin, who'd actually suffered at Stalin's hands, would join in. But he had nothing to say. They then wanted to fete him as a survivor of the tyrant's spite, but he refused and withdrew deeper into his shell. Only Ivanov sensed that the poet wasn't just being awkward; he'd suffered a hurt which went too deep for celebration.

Leykin lived in lodgings in the town and had no friends so Ivanov took him home at weekends to his village. There he spent his time wandering in the fields and the woods or playing with Alyosha, spending hours pushing the boy on a swing he'd put up under an apple tree in

Ivanov's orchard. At night he wrote into the early hours – wrote frenziedly as though at any moment the pen would be snatched from his fingers.

He rarely talked, either to Ivanov or Katerina, but they didn't find that strange. It was as though they'd always known Leykin and he was so much a part of their lives that his silence was companionable. Yet they knew nothing about him.

When the summer holidays came Ivanov felt obliged to ask the poet about his family. They themselves were off to spend a fortnight with Katerina's mother; didn't he have somebody he could visit?

Leykin shook his head. 'Nobody. My mother's dead and so is my father in a way – he's in the KGB.'

'Oh, no!' was all the dismayed Ivanov could think of saying. He'd never imagined a *zek* having a father in the secret police.

'Don't be put out,' smiled the poet, 'it has its funny side in a way. When they jugged me they jugged my old man as well. I've no idea why, but that's how our masters operate. He's been rehabilitated now and is back in the KGB, not in his old rank of course, but still pretty high up.'

'D'you ever hear from him?'

'Often – too often for my liking.' Leykin took a letter from his pocket and crumpling it into a ball he tossed it disdainfully from hand to hand. 'Here's his latest. Catch!'

Ivanov smoothed out the ball of paper. 'Dear Ilya,' he read, 'Since you never reply I've no way of knowing if you even bother to read my letters, so I must start them all the same way by saying that you are still my son and nothing, just nothing, can change my feelings for you....'

Ivanov handed the letter back to Leykin. 'I shouldn't be reading this,' he said sternly, 'and you shouldn't mock–'

'Mock!' broke in Leykin angrily. 'His whole life is a mockery! Don't you understand that it's people like my father who made it possible for Stalin to–'

He stopped, took a deep breath and continued more calmly. 'Ivan, let me try and explain. You must have been puzzled like the others when I refused to say anything against Stalin. You must have thought that for some strange reason I respected the bastard. The hell with it! He was the vilest creature our land has known. What put me off were the people abusing him. I didn't want to join in a chorus led by them because they'd been his henchmen, his tools. Without them Stalin's evil genius would have – have suppurated quietly in the Kremlin. Instead they spread his evil through the land like a contagion. And I don't mean just the KGB and the big bosses, I mean everyone who held office under Stalin – every last *apparatchik* from commissar down to local party hack.'

'But be reasonable,' protested Ivanov, 'if they were all made to pay there'd be no government, we'd drift into anarchy....'

'I'm not talking about punishment!' Leykin's voice had risen and taken on an almost ecstatic note. 'I'm talking about repentance. They must take their share of the blame. All I want them to do is acknowledge their guilt, then we can forgive them.'

'Only people like you – the people who suffered – have the right to forgive,' put in Ivanov quietly.

'Oh, no,' replied Leykin swiftly, 'that's not the point. What we suffered is of little account compared with the harm that's been done to Russia. We've all of us a right to forgive, but we can't forgive until they repent. Unless they repent we'll never rid ourselves of the evil....'

That was the theme running through all Leykin's verse. It was powerful stuff, lacerating the guilty, goading the indifferent, inspiring the innocent – a rapier thrust deep into the conscience of the nation. Some of it appeared in the literary review, 'Novy Mir,' alongside a piece by Solzhenitsyn. It was the last time either author appeared in print in Russia.

Ivanov began to fear that Leykin's days of freedom

were now being numbered. It had been convenient for the new leaders to shake a skeleton or two in the Kremlin cupboard, but opening the cupboard had turned out for them to be the opening of Pandora's box. All sorts of mischief had escaped: bankrupt words like truth and freedom had regained their solvency, and a fever of honest doubt, of earnest inquiry swept the country. Ivanov knew they'd have to put a stop to it. Any day now the box would be slammed shut and Leykin would be caught as the lid crashed down.

Before that happened Ivanov was anxious to see Leykin and his father reconciled. The old man couldn't be as bad as all that, not if he'd fathered the gentle poet. And as for the poet, Ivanov was convinced he was straining to make his mind rule his heart in this instance. Some plain speaking was called for.

'Listen to me, Ilya,' said Ivanov on the day before he left for his summer holiday, 'when I'm away I want you to promise you'll go and see your father. He's not just another apparatchik, not one of those faceless flunkeys who sent you to prison. He's your father. For all you know he might be one of those who truly regret what–'

'He's back in the KGB,' interrupted Leykin impatiently.

'He probably had no choice. Nobody leaves the KGB just when they feel like it.'

'Then he should have stayed in Siberia,' replied Leykin harshly, but Ivanov detected in his voice the beginning of a doubt.

'And what good would that do him or you or anyone? He was punished because of you. Has he ever complained about that in his letters?'

'No, but–'

'No "buts" Ilya, be honest with me. Has he ever blamed you for what happened to him?'

'No.'

'Then for pity's sake go to him. You talk about being

willing to forgive, but what is forgiveness without compassion? He must be a hurt and bewildered man, he–'

'Not him – never bewildered!' cut in Leykin, but Ivanov
ignored the interruption.

'Ilya, listen to me – listen hard. You're a lucky man,
despite all that's happened to you. You've a poet's vision,
you go through life with truth as your compass and it
takes you along a road that's crystal clear. No greys for
you, just plain black and plain white. But men like your
father have lived in the shadows all their lives, dazzled by
the white, blinded by the black, wanting to be true to
themselves perhaps, but never quite finding that road
you've found. What would they give, I wonder, to be able
to see with your eyes?'

Leykin dropped his gaze and said nothing. 'You shame
me, Ivan,' he finally muttered, 'it's your eyes they should
have, not mine. Don't worry, I'll go to see him, I promise.'

When Ivanov returned from the summer holidays there
was no Leykin. They'd come for him in the night as is
their practice and searched his room and seized his papers
and whisked him off back into that limbo from which
they'd so recently rescued him.

And in the early hours of the next day it was Ivanov's
turn. A banging on the door, the dog barking, little
Alyosha crying, Katerina's face whiter than the whitest
snow.

'You're a friend of Ilya Aleksandrovitch Leykin?'

'I am. What of it?'

'You're under arrest.'

'Why?'

'Because your friend Leykin is an enemy of the people.'

'Rubbish! He's a poet and a dreamer.'

'A so-called poet dreaming up sedition,' sneered the
man.

'Jackal!' said Ivanov.

Part Three

DEATH'S DOORWAY

18

As the winter wore on and his stock of faggots diminished alarmingly Ivanov found himself preoccupied yet again with the grim prospect of starvation.

He'd sadly miscalculated how long the faggots would last. Though he'd known from the start that there weren't enough to see him through the winter, he'd expected to bag enough hares – perhaps even another elk – to take him through to early Spring.

But the most he'd caught in two months were three hares, and though he'd found hoofprints of elk in the snow they'd led him nowhere. He doubted if he could bring down a fully grown elk with his bow and lived in hope of stumbling across the tracks of a calf.

He was afraid of extending his range of hunting any real distance from the cave in case a buran blew up. To be out one night in a blizzard would mean death. But so long as no wind was blowing the sub-zero cold was bearable and he found it surprisingly easy to move across the frozen snow, except where it had drifted.

Each time he ventured out he wrapped himself up carefully, putting on everything which was wearable – Petrisky's two shirts and trousers over his own, Petrisky's fur-lined jacket, and on top the waistcoat he'd made from the hide of the wolverine. On his head he had Petrisky's peaked hunting cap and over that a fur helmet he'd put together from the skins of hares.

He'd long ago discarded his prison boots and was wearing Petrisky's, which he lined with squirrel fur. But stout and waterproof as they were, the old man's hunting boots were not made to resist Arctic cold, and Ivanov had to knit together pelts of squirrel and suslik to make clumsy moccasins which he wore outside the boots.

When he'd first put on his winter wear he'd joked – 'I'd frighten a bear in this lot!' But it was no joke when the buran blew, the icy wind searching out gaps at neck and waist, the driven snow freezing on his moccasins, making them bags of ice.

When he was down to a week's supply of faggots Ivanov decided he must risk a long hunting trip. And no longer could he be choosy; he'd have to bag anything that moved – fox, sable, wolverine – no matter how foul the meat might taste, for he was getting perilously weak.

A faggot a day stewed with Cembra seed was all that he'd allowed himself for more than a month, and this meagre ration was now taking its toll. The strength and energy he'd built up in late summer had gone; clambering out of his bunk in the morning was now an effort of will, and once outside the cave he found he was slow to generate his own warmth. Those were danger signals he couldn't afford to ignore.

The area he chose for his hunting trip was at the base of the escarpment, some eight miles east of the cave. It was a marshy tract covered in a tall, bulrushy growth, a type of sedge which might be fodder for elk.

The night before he set out Ivanov put more charcoal than was his custom on the fire, unplugged the flue, and sat on his sable pillow, his back to the bunk. This was how he'd sat so many nights conjuring up fond images of the past, but now his thoughts were for the morrow only – the long slog in the snow, the snares he'd lay on the way, the stalking of the elk, if elk there were.

Would his luck hold up? It had been luck, not his skill nor his stamina, which had brought him so far, he told himself. The pure chance of being in the path of a squirrel migration had saved him from the first threat of starvation; then he'd literally stumbled on to his cave. A bear had killed Petrisky, who was certain to have found him otherwise. And then the fire from which he'd escaped in blind panic with only seconds to spare, had provided him with the elk without which he could not have survived the first months of winter.

Would tomorrow bring yet another reprieve? Ivanov sighed. He suddenly felt very tired and lonely. Was this the end of the road? He looked round the cave, its bare rock mellow in the glow from the fire, and marvelled for the thousandth time on its cosiness. Not a bad place to die in. When the time came it wouldn't be all that hard to snuggle into his bunk and lie there, never to get up.

19

Next morning Ivanov started out well before dawn and calculated he'd got half way to the marsh before the uncertain light of a grey day, with overcast skies, crept over the taiga. He didn't like it; the clouds were too low, the air too still. A storm was brewing.

But he plodded on, keeping a sharp lookout for spoors. His route took him under the escarpment and he stopped every half mile or so to study the rocky slopes carefully, making a mental note of every nook and cranny which might serve as a storm shelter.

When he was near the marsh he made a detour to

approach it up-wind and finished the last two hundred yards crawling through a thicket of birch. There was no elk, but his heart leapt at the sight of a maze of hoofmarks where they'd dug away the snow to get at the sedge. There were droppings too, and though they were already frozen hard Ivanov judged them to be fairly fresh. The trail left by the elks led east, away from his cave.

He wasted no time arguing the wisdom of carrying on. This was not only his last chance of finding game but his first real chance since winter started, for the spoors were fresh and the deer might be only hours away, foraging in another clearing. What clinched his decision was that some of the hoofmarks were small enough to have been made by young elk. Rogojin's bow could cope with those.

The deer trail hugged the base of the escarpment and Ivanov followed it effortlessly, sometimes breaking into a trot over the frozen snow. He'd forgotten his tiredness now and gave no thought to the miles he was putting between himself and the cave.

His caution returned only when the first flakes of snow began to fall, yet he still plodded on. There was little wind, which meant he was safe from a buran, and so long as he kept the escarpment well within view to his left, he shouldn't get lost.

Not until the elk tracks had become completely obscured by snow did he reluctantly come to a halt. By now it was snowing so hard he couldn't see for more than a few yards. He made for the escarpment and when he was among the debris of boulders at its base he settled down to the long haul home, trying not to think about what lay ahead once he was back at the cave.

He stopped once to listen when he thought he heard a clatter of hooves on the rocks of the escarpment above him. But he shook his head in disbelief; no deer could be up there.

As Ivanov peered into the grey gloom, straining to see what his commonsense told him he'd imagined, the snow fell thickly, undisturbed now by the slightest breeze, and the silence of the wilderness closed in on him. He shuddered. There was no animal anywhere near him – and no man for hundreds of miles. The enormity of his loneliness made him cringe within himself. Back in the cave he'd have cheerfully traded a human companion for a shelf of books; out here the solitude of the taiga was frighteningly primeval. Anything that lived – a dog, a cat, a tame rabbit – would now have been worth more than a library of books.

Ivanov stumbled, knocking his ankle on a boulder concealed in the snow, and the sudden pain triggered a spasm of anger which sent him half running through the snow, shouting curses, gesticulating wildly – outraged by his helplessness.

His headlong rush ended when his feet slid from under him and he lay on his back, glaring balefully into the sky, heedless of the snow falling on his face. He was rebelling, he told himself, rebelling against his ever-nagging urge to survive. Now had come the time to ask himself if the life he lived was worth striving for. To be perpetually on the brink of starvation, confined in a cave at night, spending his days in an exhausting search for food. Was that living?

Even in the summer, when hare and squirrel became fairly easy prey, he dared not relax and had to spend hours at the wearisome task of converting the meat into faggots for the winter. Every second of his waking hours was concerned with food, and now he was tired, even bored. The threat of death, being constant, had lost its edge.

Ivanov stirred uneasily. He could return to the cave, eat up his few remaining faggots, stoke up his fire and go to bed to die. But he knew he couldn't. He would continue

63

his desperate hunt for food until his last ounce of strength gave out, no matter how he felt at that moment, lying in the snow in despair.

By now the thickly falling snow had covered him completely, and he was cold and stiff. Wearily he propped himself on one elbow and as he moved he caught a glimpse of a strange shape sticking out of the rocks of the escarpment immediately above him.

He blinked the snow out of his eyes and looked again, but cautiously. His ears had already deceived him and now his eyes might be playing tricks. But what he'd seen was still there: the tail-end of an aeroplane.

As he scrambled up the cliffs he dislodged what he thought was a rock, but it turned out to be a battered tin box. It had lost its lid and was packed tight with snow, which he scooped out carefully, hoping to find some indication of what the box had contained. As he scraped the bottom he was rewarded with a handful of brown mush which could originally have been biscuits.

Excited now at the prospect of what else he might find, he jumped from ledge to ledge like a goat and hauled himself into the cleft in the cliff where the tail of the plane stuck out.

But only the tail unit was there, wedged securely in the rocks, and he realised the plane must have crashed into the cliff much higher up, its wreckage spilling over the escarpment.

He climbed higher until he reached a wide terrace, which he quartered like a hunting dog, feeling with his feet in the snow. In this way he found an engine cowling, the shattered remains of a control panel, and part of a wing which told him the plane was an army transport.

Climbing yet higher he reached a section of the escarpment which the weather had worn down into a jumble of rocky pinnacles, some four or five feet high. Jammed between two of the pinnacles and clear of the snow was a packing case, split down the middle. He fumbled inside the crack, which was packed tight with driven snow, and pulled out a tin.

For a moment Ivanov refused to believe what he held in his hand, and as he skewered the tin open with his knife he felt his whole body trembling with new hope. What he'd found was good old army tack – canned meat, a whole case of it. He sniffed cautiously at the opened tin. The meat was as good as the day it was packed.

<h2 style="text-align:center">20</h2>

It would have been easier for Ivanov had he waited until the Spring to search the wreckage further, for then the snow would have cleared from the escarpment, but he could not contain his impatience.

The first find – of canned meat – had been such a bonanza that his imagination ran wild. What other treasure had that plane been carrying? And he really meant treasure, for in no other way could he describe the meat. It had saved his life.

He salvaged 53 tins from the packing case. He had to leave behind a lot which had split open or were so battered as to become blown, but he was surprised to find so many not only intact, but unmarked. The tins were small, each weighing no more than seven ounces, but for Ivanov they represented, at half a tin a day, enough protein to keep him going for 106 days.

The plane must have crashed fairly recently, perhaps within the year, for the pieces of twisted metal he found under the snow showed no signs of rusting. The wreckage was so scattered and broken up – part of one engine was more than half a mile from the tail unit – that he concluded the plane hit the escarpment on full throttle, exploding on impact. Because of this he did not expect to find any bodies, but his scrabbling in the snow did uncover some pathetic reminders that men had died in the crash.

There was an airman's severed leg – or rather, what remained of it inside a flying boot which had been ripped open and chewed to rags by a scavenging wolf or wolverine. There was an army jacket torn to shreds, half an army cap, the stiff visor proudly uncrumpled – and most pathetic of all, a man's long johns, in strips but still recognisable, with pieces of flesh adhering to the thick wool.

The largest piece of fuselage he found was not much bigger than a small door. Carefully he marked the spot where it lay under the snow, for he was delighted to discover that the fragment of fuselage contained a port-hole which, by some freakish law of stress and strain, had survived the crash unbroken. He immediately imagined a window for his cave.

A pile of rotted sacking lying near the crate of tinned meat puzzled him until he realised this was all that remained of dozens of little bags of the sort used for packing tea and coffee. Rummaging eagerly in the sacking, hoping that perhaps a handful of coffee beans had survived, he found instead a hardened mass of yellow wax.

As he rubbed away the snow he discovered to his delight that the wax consisted of smashed candles. They must have been shattered in the crash and had then fused together in the summer sun, becoming hard again in winter. He would melt the wax, sort out the tangled pieces of wick and re-make the candles.

He had hoped to find tools, especially a saw or a spade, but concluded the plane was carrying only perishable goods. Even so, almost everything he found was useful. The thin slats of wood from the packing case containing the tinned meat made excellent patching material for the cave entrance, while the nails that had held the packing case together, though small, were worth their weight in gold.

It was on his final day of searching for wreckage that he stumbled on his strangest find. It was a wooden ammunition box, about three feet long and a foot high, reinforced by wire bands, with strap handles made of canvas, the lid fastened down by a metal clasp. It was so sturdily built that it had survived the crash intact.

The clasp was secured by a small padlock which Ivanov had to force with the blunt end of his axe. Inside were five thick packets of lined writing paper, unused, a bundle of pencils, again brand new, and two stoutly bound, bulky volumes – a copy of 'Don Quixote' in Spanish and a Spanish-Russian dictionary.

As the ammunition box was tin-lined the books and the writing paper were in perfect condition, untouched by damp.

Ivanov was puzzled. He could understand a soldier or airman using an old ammunition box for storing away his treasured mementos – medals, love letters, snapshots from home. But hardly 'Quixote', and positively not in Spanish.

There was no name or inscription on the fly leaves of either the Quixote or the dictionary and when he unwrapped the packets of writing paper he found that all the sheets were a pristine blank – waiting to be written on. But when he flipped through the pages of the Quixote a slip of paper, folded lengthwise and no doubt used as a book marker, fell out.

It was a movement order made out to a Sergeant Jablonsky. With eight men from Special Services Detachment No. 509 Sergeant Jablonsky was ordered to join Army Transport Plane FL/6429 at Omsk and provide security for – as the document cryptically put it – 'a Schedule XZ cargo destined for Vianaslav'.

Poor Jablonsky! The escarpment had turned out to be his destination, not the garrison town of Vianaslav on the Kamchatka Peninsula in Far Eastern Siberia. Sadly Ivanov surveyed the rocky escarpment where the snow now hid the shattered remains of the sergeant and his men. And of course, there was the aircrew as well, at least four men – pilot, flight engineer, navigator and radio operator. That made thirteen bodies in all. In the Spring, when the snow had gone, he would come back and build a cairn to mark their last resting place. He owed them at least that: their death had meant life for him.

Almost reverently Ivanov repacked the ammunition box, whispering his thanks to its eccentric owner. Just as the tinned meat was food for his body, so the Quixote and the paper and pencils were food for his mind. Truly that plane had brought him manna from heaven!

21

Having dragged the piece of fuselage containing a port-hole back to the cave Ivanov set about making a window.

Taking advantage of a windless day he removed three of the logs covering the entrance to the cave and chopped a foot off the top of each. When he replaced the logs he was left with a square opening roughly the size of the porthole.

Using nails from the packing case which had contained the tinned meat, he fastened the fuselage to the entrance logs, manipulating it so that the round porthole covered the square opening. To make sure no wind would dis-lodge his window he jammed two logs between the overhang and the bottom lip of the cave, driving them hard up against the fuselage.

He was delighted. Now, when the buran was blowing and he was confined to the cave, he could look out without having to unhitch his cumbersome 'door'. Also, the window relieved the feeling of being sealed off from the outside world, which was comforting at night but depressing during the day.

Next he made candles. First he melted down the solid mass of wax and unravelled the wicks. Then he made an oblong mould, using slats of wood from the packing case, and half filled the mould with melted wax.

When the wax had solidified he laid lengths of wick on top and then poured on more wax until the mould was filled. He repeated the process until he'd used up all the wax and had nearly fifty candles – clumsy, square-cut parodies of the candlemaker's skill, but they burnt with a steady flame.

His final task was to make a low writing table. For the top he again used wood from the packing case, selecting pieces with the smoothest surface. He fashioned the legs from slender, tapered branches which lent his handiwork an elegance which pleased him immensely. Ivan the dominie had surprised himself; he was fast becoming an adept carpenter!

He found that when he sat on his sable pillow facing the fire with his back resting against the bunk, he could fit the little table over his legs. He stuck a lighted candle onto the tabletop and arranged around it the Quixote, the dictionary, the writing paper and pencils. He was now ready to feast his mind.

Ivanov was glad he didn't know any Spanish, for this meant he had to read at a snail's pace, prolonging what was for him the sheer luxury of sharing another man's dreams and imaginings. He was terrified he would finish the Quixote too quickly.

The dictionary was excellent, but like most of its kind it did not give the various parts of the verbs, only the infinitives. To overcome this difficulty he skipped through the Quixote, resisting the temptation to follow the narrative and instead searched out the root forms of verbs, listing the endings for each tense and mood.

Then patiently he identified and worked out the usage of all parts of speech, noting down examples, formulating rules – and even isolating any exceptions to those rules. It was an exacting task but he responded to it with all the gusto of a spirited horse being given the rein after long confinement in a stable.

In a week he had mastered the logic of the language and then settled down to reading 'Don Quixote', not allowing himself to pass any new word without checking it in the dictionary, even though the context might have told him what it meant. Such was the pleasure the reading gave him that each evening he had to force himself to stop, otherwise he would have carried on until morning.

Those were happy nights. Outside the buran howled across the icy wastes, tearing at the trees of the darkened taiga, sending flurries of freezing snow spattering against his little window. And inside he sat with book and candle, his charcoal fire blazing merrily, his mind a thousand miles away, wandering the dusty plains of the Mancha.

22

Though he now had his store of canned meat Ivanov did not relax his efforts with bow and snare. Only two days after finding the plane he was high up on the escarpment searching for more wreckage when he saw a group of elk foraging in a clearing below him.

He was amazed at his own stupidity in not appreciating until now the value of the escarpment as a look-out place. With the clearings blanketed in snow anything that moved and which was not fitted with a white winter coat caught the eye. Using pencil and paper from the ammunition box he mapped out the clearings and any marshy tracts within hunting distance of his cave. His idea was to plan his trips from now on and not just blunder through the taiga hoping to stumble on good hunting terrain.

Perhaps it was because he was more relaxed now that he had a reserve of food to fall back on, or perhaps because at last he was applying a thought-out method to his hunting, but whatever the reason he began to bag so much game that he was hardly a day without fresh meat.

He picked up the track of a young elk in one clearing and thanks to his map could anticipate its movements by running ahead to the next clearing where he lay in wait, felling it with an arrow from his bow at a range of only ten feet.

In the marshy tracts he prepared deer snares made out of running nooses of rabbit wire which he suspended from the boughs of trees. Up to now he had used the wire for trapping hares only and though he doubled the wire for the deer he realised it was not strong enough to hold a sizeable elk. So he strung the nooses low in the hope of catching calves. It almost shocked him to find how effectively his snares worked. In three days he caught two calves.

But hare was his favourite meat. Up to now he had laid snares wherever he found a track and it was rare that he caught anything. So he adopted a different tactic, ignoring the single tracks until he had traced them back into doubles, and then following the doubles down to multiples until he was on what he called the 'trunk track' – a well-beaten path in the snow, almost a highway for hares. This took time and sometimes he lost the tracks al-

71

together where the snow had drifted, but the extra effort resulted in a dramatic improvement in his supply of hare meat.

Conserving the fresh meat was no problem, all he had to do was leave it out in the snow. To prevent wolverines getting at it he built a squat bunker or box made of logs lashed together with birch bark. He put the meat inside, covered it with snow and placed heavy logs on top, criss-crossed in two layers. Only a bear could have got at the meat, but bears were now deep in hibernation.

On the day when Ivanov returned from the hunt to find that his day's kill topped up the bunker so that it was full to the brim with fresh meat he felt he could fairly claim having beaten the taiga. And when he looked back he was amazed that he should have been so despondent at times.

There was no question now of his wondering if the effort of survival was worth the sort of life it gave him. It was brutish, though the 'Quixote' and the dictionary had leavened the arid routine of coping with his purely physical needs. But what mattered to him most was being his own master, for it was to regain the responsibilities of freedom that he had escaped. If he were to die in the wilderness it would be because of his own inadequacy. He would not be dying at the whim of a prison guard or because the prison authorities overworked him and failed to feed him.

And, of course, in addition to that he always had at the back of his mind the hope of reunion with Katerina. There might not be the remotest chance of it, for if he survived the taiga and broke through to the settled areas of Siberia, he would be risking recapture in every mile of the thousand miles to Katerina. But the mere thought of seeing her again sustained him daily. Even now he was looking forward to the Spring when once again he would resume his trek south, to be that much nearer to her.

23

It was perhaps well that at this time of high hope Ivanov could not see himself. In the summer he had studied the reflection of his emaciated features in the river pools while fishing so he would have been prepared for his ravaged look, but not the deep-sunk staring eyes, the peeling lips, the blistered skin on cheeks, nose and brow. And ironically, this change had been wrought in the weeks of plenty, when hunting was good and he ended each day with a full belly.

As Spring approached, Ivanov could not help noticing how his hair was coming out, but he felt so fit he chose to ignore it. And then suddenly, as though overnight, his teeth were loose. He was horrified when a gentle tug brought a tooth clean out of the gum, painlessly and bloodlessly.

He knew then there was something radically wrong, and when a tremor of the head, so slight he ignored it at first, spread to his arms and legs, he became frightened. Yet he did not feel ill: there was no pain, no weakness.

It could not be scurvy, for he had seen enough of that in the prison camp to know his gums should be bleeding and he should feel agonisingly weak. And though losing his hair and teeth was worrying enough, that could be put down to a vitamin deficiency of some sort. What frightened him was the tremor. Had he suffered a stroke without knowing it?

The answer came with the thaw when Ivanov decided he could now fulfil his promise and build a cairn for the dead soldiers and airmen. The escarpment was already almost clear of snow and it would be easy to collect enough boulders for a quite imposing monument.

As he approached the terrace where he had found the engine cowling and part of a wing he was surprised to see that the ground all round was brown and bare. Other terraces were already mistily green with the sprouting of the quick Spring grass, and boulders elsewhere were sprinkled with moss and lichen. But here nothing grew.

The barren patch, he noticed, ran down the escarpment like an ugly stain nearly a quarter of a mile wide, ending up in the taiga far below. Where it had spread away from the base of the escarpment the trees were dead, the foliage still intact, but brown and withered.

A sudden nausea seized Ivanov and he fell to his knees gagging. His head was whirling and his eyes stinging, as if lashed by ammonia. He staggered back the way he had come, trying to run across the bare ground, but finding it difficult now to breathe.

When he reached a group of pines still green and well to windward of the bare patch he fell to the ground, doubled up by another bout of violent retching. As this passed he found he could not keep still, his arms and legs jerking spasmodically, his head twitching from side to side.

How long he lay there he did not know, for he must have fainted and it was almost dark when he came to. The twitching had ceased and the wretched nausea had left him, but he felt limp, hollowed out, as though drained of blood and warmth.

Shivering with cold he staggered loose-kneed through the early night, swaying like a drunk, the warmth and comfort of his cave a beacon in his mind.

'Don't worry, Ivan my boy, you'll make it,' he reassured himself. 'Just a bad bout of 'flu. After a good night's rest you'll be as right as rain in the morning.'

He stopped as he said this, tears pricking his eyes. He

74

wanted to weep, not out of self-pity, but for pity of this other self, this Ivan the Indomitable who would not accept defeat, who sought to ignore the convulsions and the nausea, the loose teeth and the falling hair.

What dreadful contagion had he picked up from the wreckage of that plane? He recalled the sinister reference to a 'Schedule XZ cargo' in Jablonsky's movement order – a cargo so important it had rated a security guard of one sergeant and eight men. It must have been a top secret chemical, probably packed in containers which exploded when the plane crashed. Canned virus, that was it – a new monster from the biological warfare laboratories. Ivan shuddered.

All those days he had spent searching for wreckage in the snow he had been breathing in the poison, getting it on his hands and clothes – and even eating it, for no doubt he had contaminated the canned meat when he opened the tins.

If only he had discovered the wreckage in summer he would have been immediately warned by the choking gases rising from the scorched ground – as had happened that morning. But in winter the poison percolated through the snow, an insidious, undetectable contamination.

When he reached the cave his one thought was to make up the fire, but he was strangely clumsy, his hands seeming to have a life of their own, refusing the commands of his brain.

By the time he had the fire going he was almost prostrate with exhaustion and the very thought of the effort involved in undoing his outdoor clothing appalled him. So he stretched out in front of the fire fully clothed. He was afraid to clamber into his bunk in case he became too weak to get out again. Through the mist of fatigue which clogged his mind there came the thought that it was not yet time to die.

24

When Ivanov awoke the light of a bright day poured in
through his little window. He lay still, wondering where
he was.

It could have been the attic at home, where they stored
the apples, laid out on brown paper spread over the floor.
He must be careful how he moved. Katerina would be
annoyed if he crushed any of the apples.

Or was he in the prison hospital? That was cold and
gloomy, with just one window high up the wall. He had
fallen on the ice and broken a rib. It didn't hurt now
because they had bound him up and told him to lie
perfectly still. He had better not move, not just yet.

But what was that? His heart leapt. It was little Alyosha
calling him. How stupid of him to waste his time like this,
lying on his back in the orchard, looking up at the sky
through the trees when he could have been playing with
the boy.

'I'm coming!' he shouted and rose on one elbow. A
wave of nausea engulfed him and he lay back, breathing
hard, fighting not to retch. He knew now where he was: in
the cave and mortally sick.

The fire had long gone out and the cave was cold.
Bracing himself on both arms he cautiously sat up. If he
moved ever so slowly he might beat the attacks of nausea,
and he had to get that fire going again at all costs.

Not daring to stand up he crawled into the corner of the
cave where he had stacked the charcoal and some dried
timber. Trembling with the effort he dragged a pile of the
fuel next to the fireplace and then by a supreme effort of

will managed to control his fumbling fingers long enough to strike a spark with the tinder box.

When he had the fire going he lit a candle and placed all his other candles beside it. If the fire went out again he would have a burning candle to light it with. His hands were swiftly becoming useless and he knew he could not cope again with the flint and wheel of the tinder box.

He had left some stew of hare and Cembra seed in his little cauldron and he heated this over the fire. The very thought of food repelled him, but unless he ate he would lose what little strength he had left. He managed to force down a spoonful of the stew and promptly vomited it. He tried again, but this brought on another attack of the agonising retching.

For the rest of that day he lay by the fire, staring at the window until the last hint of daylight had left it. So long as he lay still the nausea did not bother him and he was in no pain. His arms and legs felt cold, but not uncomfortably so; it was more of a numbness.

Though he tried to resist the thought of death he could not help wondering if someone might not stumble on his cave in years to come and discover his remains. He must leave a message for Katerina. She might be an old woman before she got it, but he must tell her he loved her to the end.

Ivanov crawled over to the ammunition box and took out some sheets of writing paper. By holding one hand on the other to steady it he managed to scrawl in pencil, in shaky capitals:

'For Katerina Semyonovna Ivanov, of Veshenskaya on the Don, from her husband, Ivan Mikailovitch Ivanov. I love you. Kiss Alyosha for me and–'

He failed to finish, collapsing over the ammunition box, his head whirling in a vortex of fatigue which threatened to plunge him into unconsciousness.

Crawling back to the fire he found he was dragging his legs. He had lost all feeling in them and he was afraid his arms, now numb from shoulder to elbow, would soon fail him as well.

He looked with longing at the bunk. There he would be warm even when the fire went out, and unless he got in now when he still had the use of his arms he would never manage it.

He banked up the fire with timber and charcoal and dragged his writing table next to the bunk. The bucket he had so laboriously carved out of a log and which he used for storing water was too heavy to lift onto the table, so filled his tin mug and put this on the table instead. He could not swallow even water without gagging, but he had a burning thirst and he found he could ease it by swilling his mouth out.

He next lit all his candles and stuck them as securely as he could on the tabletop. He could not endure the thought of dying in the dark – if he were to die. And he had more grease to make more candles should he survive.

His head felt cold so he put on his helmet of hare pelts, wrapped his wolverine waistcoat about him tight with a thong of deer hide, and dragged himself into his bunk.

As he sank back into the soft birch leaves, his head on the sable pillow, an almost ecstatic feeling of relief coursed through his body, relaxing even the aching muscles of his stomach, racked by the violent retching. He felt himself drifting into sleep and it was as much as he could do to pull Petrisky's sleeping bag over him before his eyes closed.

25

When he awoke it was still dark outside and he wondered if he would last out the night. The numbness in his legs had spread to his groin, his arms lay inert and useless beneath the sleeping bag and he could no longer move his head.

Which would go first, he wondered, his brain or his lungs? If the paralysis reached his brain first, that would be a quick, painless death. But the lungs could mean a slow suffocation.

He was surprised he could think so rationally and be so calm. He should be frightened, he told himself, but instead he felt wonderfully untroubled lying there, looking at the guttering candles, listening to the wind. It was the wind of early summer, gentle, lamenting, not the furious buran of mid-winter.

And how that buran had blown! Yet, he had beaten it and the taiga, too. If only Rogojin knew, how proud he would be of four-thumbed Ivan! Ivanov's lips creased in a stiff smile at the thought.

He would have been on his way south now, a seasoned traveller in the taiga, a master of the wilderness but for that confounded plane. That thought had convulsed him with bitterness when he first realised how ill he was and he had become engulfed in self-pity, asking himself despairingly why he should be singled out for such a cruel slice of ill-fortune.

But now, at death's door, he felt no resentment. A veil seemed to have dropped and he saw with crystal clarity that destiny was neither cruel nor kind; only human frailty judged it so.

What mattered was to rise above what happened to him and master it, not just by stoically accepting the inevitable, but by fighting it to the last, by refusing to be defeated.

'Face death squarely,' he told himself grimly, 'but don't accept it – defy it!'

He sighed. It would have been so easy to give in, to let go his feeble hold on life and drift gently into oblivion. No animal urge to survive sustained him now. Death no longer terrorised; it tempted.

'Damn you, death!' he shouted. His voice was a feeble croak, but within him it had the sound of thunder. 'I'll fight you every inch of the way!' And Ivanov knew that to die would be no defeat, for each breath he now breathed would be a victory, each moment of self-awareness snatched from the void engulfing his dying mind would be a battle won.

He closed his eyes. A soothing warmth, like sunshine in April, bathed his face and a voice calling him on the wind came nearer and nearer. It was Alyosha, but not an Alyosha blurred by the frenzy of his illness. The boy was with him now in a clarity of recall so vivid it became for Ivanov reality.

Through his closed eyelids he watched the smiling boy bending over him.

'Get up lazybones, get up and come and play!'

And they ran together hand-in-hand to where Katerina was waiting, arms outstretched. She kissed him and held his face in her cupped hands.

'Ivan, oh Ivan – you've come home!'

Part Four

TREK SOUTH

26

It might have been hours later, it might have been days –
Ivanov was never to know – but when next he opened his
eyes he found himself looking up into a shaft of golden
light. He felt the warmth of the light steal through him,
reaching the very marrow of his bones. He sighed and
asked himself almost contentedly, 'Is this then the way
death comes?'

A voice answered feebly but urgently. It was his own,
nagging at him as though from the edge of oblivion.
'Don't give in now! You've won – you've won!'

That brought him fully to his senses. The shaft of light
was the sun shining through the porthole window of his
cave, pouring its life-giving warmth into his bunk. He felt
rested and at ease, as though he had slept long and deeply
after a hard day's hunting. Gone were the stomach
cramps and the nausea. Gone too was the appalling
weariness which had seemed to gnaw at his vitals.

'I'm better!' he marvelled, 'and I can move!' He flexed
his fingers, then gripped the sides of the bunk. He twid-
dled his toes and bent his knees. He was still weak, but
there was no sickening giddiness; his head and hands no
longer shook.

Then he remembered the vision of his wife and child. It
had been so vivid he could still feel the touch of
Katerina's fingers on his face. He opened his right hand

and kissed the palm, for in it lingered the warmth of Alyosha's chubby little fist. They had saved him, they had pulled him back from the brink of death.

A sob escaped him, then his wasted frame shook as he bent forward in his bunk and wept for sheer joy. Not only was he alive but Katerina and Alyosha were closer to him now than at any time since he'd been torn away from them. New hope welled within him. 'I'm coming home, my dears!' he declared through his tears, 'nothing can stop me now, not after what I've been through. I'm coming home!'

Ivanov's recovery was swift. He ate carefully to begin with, keeping to stewed hare and not risking the stronger flavoured squirrel and venison stored in the bunker outside the cave. His stomach was still queasy.

Before each meal he drank a mug of tea made from spruce needles. Rogojin had told him that the needles of the spruce tree were high in ascorbic acid and were used as a cure for scurvy. While he knew only too well that he was getting over an illness infinitely worse than scurvy, he thought that an infusion brewed from the needles might act as a much-needed tonic. He was right. The tea not only stimulated his appetite, but whenever the dreadful nausea of his illness threatened to return he found that he could keep it at bay with a mugful of what he came to call his 'lifesaver'.

When he was fit enough to be tempted by the thought of a chunk of roebuck roasting on the spit over his fire, he decided he was fit enough to start hunting again. There was still meat in his bunker, but the winter cold which had served as such an effective refrigerator was now giving way to the first warm flush of summer and he couldn't risk upsetting his stomach by eating meat which was high.

He realised he'd have to carry the stale meat well away from the cave – dump it in the conduit at the far end of the lake probably – but he put off doing it from day to day. He just couldn't bring himself to waste food which had been so hardly won in the bitter winter months. A few days later he was to rejoice he hadn't after all dumped the rejected meat; he found a hungry mouth which consumed every last scrap of it.

He was out examining snares he'd laid in the new grass on the lower terraces of the escarpment when he heard a plaintive mewing sound. Thinking a hare had been caught and not killed outright by a snare, he hurried to deliver the coup de grâce and almost trod on a wolf cub.

It was half hidden in a tumble of loose rocks where drifting snow still defied the early summer sun. The cub stopped whimpering when it saw Ivanov and pressed itself close to the rocks. It was so thin that the outline of its skeleton could be seen through the wet fur and its eyes were protruding from the skull. It was too weak to flee, but when Ivanov picked it up it made a pathetic attempt to bare its teeth and snarl.

27

Back at the cave Ivanov dried the cub before the fire and wrapped it in his wolverine waistcoat. It was too young to have been weaned so Ivanov prepared a soup from the remains of his morning's meal of stewed hare and hoped the pup would think it was milk. But it turned its head from the spoon, jaw clamped shut.

Then Ivanov remembered reading somewhere – or had the all-knowing Rogojin told him? – that mother wolves fed regurgitated meat to their cubs while they were still suckling them. He chewed away at a mouthful of hare meat and then spat it into his hand. The cub's response was electric. It nuzzled at Ivanov's hand and gulped down the meat, then licked at his palm for more.

That was the beginning of a feeding ritual which Ivanov kept up for a week – four times a day and twice in the night. The cub grew before his eyes, filling out from head to tail like a little balloon. At the end of the week it was eating the raw meat from the bunker and romping round the cave – as playful and mischievous as the puppy of any domesticated dog.

But not for a moment did Ivanov pretend to himself that he could keep the pup as a pet and he made no attempt to restrict its movements, allowing it to leave the cave when it wished. He knew that after a few months more, when it could fend for itself, the cub would wander away and not return.

Until that happened he intended enjoying its company to the full. He found that if he stroked the cub or in any way handled it caressingly it would cringe and struggle to escape his hold, but when he cuffed it playfully or gripped it roughly by the throat it became frantic with delight, reacting so boisterously that Ivanov had to beware of its needle-sharp teeth.

And those teeth became a problem. How could he teach the pup not to bite too hard? A sharp blow or a smack too severe to be part of the play routine would only have confused and frightened the animal. So he did what its mother would have done: he bit it. Holding its head firmly between his hands he gave its ear a sharp nip. The puppy yelped in pain but didn't run away; instead it licked at Ivanov's face placatingly.

When Ivanov threw sticks and stones for the cub it gave chase eagerly like any other puppy, but it then disappeared and never returned with what had been thrown. This puzzled Ivanov until he chanced on a cache of sticks and stones hidden among the boulders near the cave. Also in the cache were odd items he had mislaid since the cub had been with him – an old spoon made from birchwood, the leather thong from his wolverine waistcoat and three wooden pegs he used in laying snares.

Ivanov soon realised that anything he touched and then discarded found its way to the secret lair among the boulders.

He put this to the test when he was with the pup on the shingle terraces at the edge of the lake, a half mile or more from the cave. Carefully selecting a distinctively coloured pebble from the unnumbered thousands at his feet, he rubbed it between his palms and replaced it while the cub was distracted by a carrion crow. When he next visited the cache the coloured pebble was there.

Obviously the pup treasured anything with Ivanov's scent on it. He told himself it must be instinctive behaviour of some sort and had nothing to do with affection. But he felt flattered and his heart warmed to the little creature.

It was a bitch and true to her wolf nature she never barked. But when excited she made an abrupt hissing sound in her throat which came out like 'So-so'.

'And how are you this morning?' Ivanov would gravely inquire, and to his delight the cub seemed to answer, 'So, so'. Inevitably he christened her 'So-so', but no matter how often he repeated the name she failed to answer to it. When Ivanov wanted So-so to come to him he made the sharp 'Tsick, tsick!' sound he'd heard old Petrisky make to the half wild hunting dogs back at the prison camp. It worked right from the start, So-so slinking up to him with her tail tight between her legs, as though responding against her instincts to a call she just could not resist.

28

Ivanov was to remember those early days of summer as an idyllic time. He was so adept now at hunting and trapping that game seemed to fall into his hands, and he was strong again, his muscles responding effortlessly to the raw physical challenge which was his daily lot.

But more important was his state of mind. He was at peace with himself, convinced now that he had done right to escape and confident that he could not only beat the taiga but survive to take up his life again with Katerina and Alyosha.

How that was to be he had no idea until one morning, while fishing in the lake, Ivanov caught the reflection of his face in the water. Lugubriously he noted his almost toothless mouth and his completely bald pate. Even his eyebrows were gone.

'What a scarecrow!' he exclaimed, 'not even Katerina would recognise me!' Then he corrected himself. Katerina would know him, no matter how he looked, and he knew the change in him would make no difference to her. It was others who wouldn't recognise him. Even his best friend back home, Jacob Bagritsky the biology teacher, would have to look twice.

'That's it!' he shouted, dropping his fishing line in his excitement. Identity was the key; he must exploit his changed appearance. But how?

He began to pace the shingle beside the lake, sending up showers of pebbles as he vigorously about-turned, scaring away poor So-so who had never seen her mild-mannered master in such a stern mood.

'If I just make up a new identity they'd catch me out in

no time,' he told himself, 'because all they'd have to do is check me against their records.' No, he'd have to pick on a real person, preferably somebody recently dead. The unfortunate Jablonsky, who had been in charge of the security men on board the plane, came immediately to mind. Ivanov even had the sergeant's movement order, which was an official document – a proof of identity.

But for how long could he keep up the pretence? He knew nothing about Jablonsky and even if he survived the initial questioning he'd be given short shrift by the dead man's family.

Ivanov stopped his pacing and stared unseeing across the lake. Try as he might he couldn't find a way of using Jablonsky so as to give himself a new identity, and yet he sensed that there was something significant about the sergeant or his movement order or the plane itself which bored right into the core of his problem. What was it?

As he stood by the lake lost in thought he became suddenly aware of the warmth of the midday sun. The summer was galloping by and here he was still in his winter quarters when he should be on his way south.

'I must get moving,' he told himself. 'I can do all this thinking on the march.' Indeed, the challenge of a long trek might sharpen his wits and bring him the solution which now so tantalisingly evaded him. 'It's something simple!' he exclaimed impatiently, 'so simple that it's staring me in the face and I can't see it!'

It was with mixed feelings that Ivanov abandoned his winter quarters. The cave had witnessed the trials and triumphs of his battle with the taiga, and apart from his boyhood home he had never before become so physically intimate with a place. But it reminded him too of his dreadful illness. He was sorry to leave and at the same time deeply thankful he was able to leave.

It was too much to hope that he'd stumble across another cave so ideally suited to his needs, but that no longer worried Ivanov. By now he was skilled enough with Petrisky's axe to be able to build himself a weather-proof shelter from logs. But to avoid having to start another winter home from scratch he decided to take with him everything which could conceivably be of any use.

This made a load too heavy to carry. Another drag pole was the answer – of the sort he'd used to transport his elk meat the autumn before. But this time he cut himself a log which forked at both ends. One end fitted round his shoulders like a yoke and was strapped into place with strips of rawhide. The other fork rested squarely on the ground and prevented the log from rolling. So that the log would slide smoothly he whittled away at the ends of the fork until they took the shape of sledge runners. This was a vast improvement on his original drag pole, and when he tried it out he was surprised that so simple a contrivance could be made to carry a heavy load so smoothly.

Encouraged by his success with the drag pole Ivanov decided to make a tent so that when he camped down at the end of the day he could be sure of getting a dry night's sleep. He thought of using the skins he'd collected during the winter, but found they had dried too quickly in the warmth of the cave and were now like panels of plywood. He had to make do with the bear skin he'd used as a rug on the floor of the cave and the roebuck skin which had served as a curtain. He stitched them together to make a canopy and then constructed a folding framework of willow sticks. He sat back on his heels to survey his handiwork – and nearly broke a rib laughing. His 'tent' looked for all the world like a crumpled old bear wearing a skirt of buckskin! So-so decided it was alive and re-treated to a safe distance, growling and spitting. It was ages before she could be tempted inside.

Ivanov started off with an ample reserve of faggots,

which meant he didn't have to stop to hunt, contenting himself with a snared hare when he felt in need of fresh meat.

He walked from dawn until almost dusk – fifteen hours a day – but took care not to overtire himself, halting frequently for snacks and a brew-up of his spruce tea which had become by now a mild addiction.

On the very first day he found his pace too gruelling for So-so. She of course covered two miles for every one of his, darting off excitedly into the woods, on the trail of scents which led her nowhere. She became so exhausted that Ivanov had to put her in Petrisky's haversack, which he was carrying slung from one shoulder.

He had to smile at the thought of somebody seeing him plodding laboriously between the trees, dragging the pole with its hefty burden, his bald head glistening with sweat, his once full beard now reduced to bristly tufts since his illness, his jacket and trousers patched in squirrel fur – and peeping from the haversack swinging at his side the bright eyes of a young wolf!

29

Marching all day under the sun of full summer was hot work. He had packed onto the drag pole his fur headgear and winter boots, together with the wolverine waistcoat and other pieces of pelt clothing he had made for winter wear. On his feet were the moccasins he'd stitched from squirrel and suslik hides. They made easy walking and stood up surprisingly well to the daily slog.

Petrisky's hunting cap was too heavy to wear in the hot sun and he sorely missed a light floppy hat to protect his head and face from the clouds of midges which infested the taiga in the summer. Before his illness his thick hair and beard had been sufficient protection.

After a month's marching he noticed subtle changes in the terrain. The forest of spruce and fir seemed to be the same, stretching away endlessly on all sides, but the grassy clearings became larger. Sometimes he found himself in woods composed entirely of birch – tall, strong-growing trees, quite unlike the stunted birch of the far north.

But what struck him most forcibly was the comparative dryness underfoot. He had become used to ploughing his way through bog and marsh and bedding down on the slushy debris of forest floors where the water never completely drained away because of the solid permafrost a few feet below the surface. Now he was surprised to find that streams had become infrequent and one night when he made camp he had to search around for water – the first time that had happened to him.

As the days went by he sensed that the ground was rising imperceptibly and when he climbed a tall spruce to get the lay of the land ahead he could see a line of low hills, blue in the distance.

That confirmed what he'd thought for some days: he was crossing an immense watershed – a wilderness of forest stretching for hundreds of miles – which lay in between the main river system where the new towns and settlements had been built.

What should he do: carry straight on into the un-explored taiga or head for the settled areas to the east or west? His every instinct urged him to strike west, in the general direction of home, but he wondered if he'd come far enough south.

Perhaps it would be safer for him to cross the water-shed, even if it meant spending the winter on it. In that case he'd have to hurry to get south of the hills before the summer ended. He didn't fancy a winter on the north facing slope, slight as it was. The unbroken force of the buran would sweep it from end to end.

It was still early in the day but he decided to make camp where he was. He'd sleep on the problem and see how he felt in the morning.

While gathering sticks for his fire he couldn't fail to notice an abundance of deer marks; he was in good hunting country.

The thought of deer reminded him it was a long time since he'd tasted venison. Why shouldn't he indulge himself this once and bag a buck for dinner? He'd walked steadily, day after day, for more than a month. Wasn't it time he gave himself a break?

First he had to tie up So-so. She was still too boisterous for a hunt and would scare away all the deer for miles around. There was no point in leaving her on a leash, for she'd bite through the toughest leather thongs in seconds. So he tied her legs together and then put her in a small buckskin bag up to her neck, fastening the bag securely to the main support pole inside his tent.

Terrified by this new experience, the puppy whined and whimpered and when Ivanov was nearly half a mile away he could still hear her plaintive cry. It tugged at his heart but did not worry him. She was perfectly safe, for his little tent was so heavily impregnated with his scent that no animal, not even the intrepid wolverine, would dare enter it. And that was how Ivanov came to make a grievous error; he forgot about man.

30

Unharnessed from the drag pole and exhilarated by the feeling of freedom this gave him, Ivanov broke into a brisk jogtrot as he followed the deer spoors, dodging in and out of the trees as silently as a shadow.

After his exacting apprenticeship stalking elk in the snows of the far north, tracking down these southern deer was child's play. He didn't realise that he had now become as competent a hunter as any of the taiga predators.

When he caught up with the deer they were browsing in a glade upwind of him and he was able to approach so near he could hear an old cow grinding her worn molars as she chewed away at the tender leaves of young birch.

He picked out the smallest of the bucks and downed it where it stood, his arrow piercing the jugular and reaching down into the animal's heart. It was the cleanest kill he'd ever made with his bow. How proud poor Rogojin would have been of him now!

With the buck wrapped round his neck he was almost in sight of his camp when a sound he hadn't heard since dodging Petrisky's patrol more than a year before stopped him in his tracks. Human voices!

Dropping the buck he moved through the trees until he was on the edge of the little clearing where he had erected his tent. Two men were there, one bearded and heavily built, wearing the leather waistcoat, fur hat and high boots of a trapper. The other, taller and clean shaven, wore an elegant hunting jacket of fine wool, with buttoned pockets and leather patches at the elbows. He was holding a shotgun and leaning over the tent as his companion thrust a hand inside and dragged out So-so.

'I can't believe it – it's a wolf!' exclaimed the trapper. He took So-so out of the buckskin bag and then dropped her smartly. 'She's bitten me!' he yelled, sucking at his thumb and then waving his hand in the air as if to cool it. Ivanov had to smile. Even from where he crouched in the underbrush some fifty yards away he'd heard the sharp click of the cub's teeth as she snapped. He was the only man allowed to handle her!

Then he stopped smiling. He shouldn't have left the cub in the tent. It was her whining which had attracted the men to the clearing and now he was in a proper fix. What if the men searched his baggage?

Ivanov had planned to get rid of everything which could connect him with the prison camp, including even his underclothes. There was also the dead Petrisky's gear to be thrown away. At that very moment he was wearing the old man's jacket which was regulation issue for prison guards. He groaned. These men had taken him completely by surprise.

'Eh, look at this!' Ivanov's heart sank. It was the man in the fancy hunting jacket who had shouted and he was pulling Ivanov's blanket from inside the tent. His prison number was stencilled on it in yellow dye.

The two men huddled over the blanket, running it through their hands and talking excitedly. Then the trapper pulled roughly at the little tent, wrenching it free from its framework of willow sticks, while his companion stood up and looked round, obviously searching.

Ivanov had left the drag pole, with its load still tied to it, beneath the branches of a fallen tree which lay beside the tent. He'd made no real attempt at concealing it and he knew the man would spot it at any moment.

A sudden curse switched his attention back to the

trapper. He had Petrisky's sleeping bag in one hand and was hopping around holding his ankle with the other. 'That blasted wolf!' he bellowed, 'she's gone and bitten my foot!'

The tall man laughed and this seemed to infuriate the trapper, for he took a sudden kick at the bound cub. Ivanov made to stand up, a protesting yell rising in his throat, but before he could either move or make a sound So-so was free and running across the clearing towards him. The trapper's kick had sent her rolling and this must have loosened the thongs which bound her legs.

'Get her, shoot her down!' screamed the trapper. He'd left a hunting rifle leaning against the trunk of the fallen tree and he now made a dash for it. But the tall man hadn't put down his shotgun. In one swift but unhurried movement he swung round on his heels, took aim and fired.

As the shot rang out So-so stumbled but next moment was in the shelter of the trees and Ivanov dropped to his knees, expecting her to come bounding up to him. He was upwind of her and she must have picked up his scent, he was sure of that. He crawled through the underbrush and there she was, still struggling valiantly to reach him, but with her hind legs ripped to shreds by buckshot.

He cradled her in his arms and she licked his face, her yellow wolf eyes wide with pain. He examined her wounds and groaned helplessly. There was nothing he could do; her legs were shattered and some of the buckshot had ripped into her belly.

Cupping her head gently in his left hand he drew his hunting knife with his right. 'And how is my puppy this morning?' he murmured soothingly. The familiar greeting seemed to reach through the cub's pain. 'So, so,' she responded bravely, making the hissing sound in her throat which was her only way of showing affection. Ivanov's knife cut through her heart in one clean thrust and she died with her gaze fixed on him trustingly.

As Ivanov staggered to his feet a wild rage blinded him. Why had they killed his little wolf? What sort of mindless brutes were these men?

'Butchers!' he screamed. 'Assassins!'

The man in the hunting jacket was walking across the clearing to the spot where So-so had leapt into the underbrush. He now stopped and scanned the woods to left and right, bringing up his shotgun menacingly.

'You out there!' he shouted imperiously, 'you out there in the woods, move into the open so that I can see you!'

Ivanov blinked away his tears of grief and rage and shook his head incredulously. Was this oaf in his fancy hunting jacket now giving him orders?

'Puppy killer!' His anger choked him. 'I'll make you pay for this!'

'Enough of that!' The man's tone was more imperious than ever. 'I'm an officer of the armed forces and I'm arresting you on suspicion of being an escaped prisoner. Move out into the open or I'll flush you out!' He aimed his shotgun and held it steady on the spot where he judged Ivanov to be.

The words 'arresting' and 'prisoner' cut like an ice-cold knife through the hot rage befogging Ivanov's mind. Was this then the end of the road? Had his striving against the taiga, his courage and stamina in resisting starvation and illness, his high hopes for freedom – had it all been in vain?

Another surge of anger shook Ivanov, but now it was the anger of despair. He wasn't going to surrender meekly, not to anyone and least of all to these two villains who had coldly killed his wolf cub. He'd endured too much. If this was the end of the road, then it was the end of his life. He was *not* going to be taken prisoner again.

'Listen, butcher!' he shouted. His voice was no longer thick with rage, it rang clear and menacing. 'If you fire that gun again, you die! D'you hear me? You die!'

The man lowered his shotgun, for a moment uncertain. He turned to the trapper who was now standing beside him and muttering something. The trapper grinned and nodded vigorously.

Turning back in Ivanov's direction the man raised his shotgun again. 'If that's the way you want it,' he shouted, 'we'll come and get you!' With that he fired and dropped to the ground, rolling swiftly out of sight behind a fallen tree. At the same time the trapper, bent double and jinking like a startled hare, ran to the far side of the clearing and plunged into the woods.

Ivanov heard the buckshot whistle through the foliage around him, but he paid it scant attention. His eyes were on the clearing. The way these men moved told him they had worked together before; he'd taken on a couple of experts.

31

Weighing the odds against him Ivanov decided he needn't worry too much about the shotgun; his bow could match it fairly, though he'd have to watch out for the scatter effect of buckshot. But the trapper had a hunting rifle – a long-range weapon fitted with telescopic sights. If the trapper got a bead on Ivanov he'd be able to pick him off without having to come anywhere near him.

He moved deeper into the woods, but not too far from the edge of the clearing, which still showed up as a belt of light in the gloom of the forest. He felt sharply alert, as though all his senses had been switched into top gear. 'I must get them to come to me,' he reasoned, 'because my only chance against that hunting rifle is an ambush at close quarters, well within range of my bow.'

Taking off his jacket he re-buttoned it and stuffed it with debris from the forest floor, ramming twigs down the sleeves and jamming broken branches crosswise inside the chest and waist. He propped the dummy against a tree, wrapping the arms around a low branch and partly concealing it in foliage.

Ivanov stepped back and smiled grimly. In the poor light of the woods his dummy looked like a man crouched in the firing position behind the cover of a tree.

Not taking his eyes off the dummy Ivanov then backed away for thirty feet, making sure he maintained a straight line of fire through the tangle of trees and underbrush. Unlike a bullet his arrow could be deflected by the lightest twig.

When he reached a thicket of brambles he burrowed into it, not feeling the thorns which scratched at his face and hands.

He crouched low, the brambles pressing in on him from all sides. He checked the arrows in his rawhide quiver and carefully selected two which had proved truest in flight. He fitted one arrow into the bowstring and the other he gripped between his teeth. He didn't count on having to use more than two; if he had to, he'd stand no chance against the counter-fire of a shotgun or rifle.

Ivanov didn't hear them come. The woods were perfectly still, not the slightest hint of a breeze ruffling the foliage. He was sure he'd hear something in that silence – the crackle of a twig, the swish of clothing, even their breathing. But the first he knew they'd arrived was when a sharp report seemed to explode almost in his ear. At the same second his dummy spurted dust and collapsed at the foot of the tree.

Ivanov froze, not daring to move – not even to draw his

bow. The trapper was right behind him, just on the other side of his thicket of brambles.

'Got him?' It was the man Ivanov had come to think of as Fancy Jacket who was speaking. His voice came from ahead of Ivanov, slightly to the right.

'No, he rigged up a decoy, keep your head down.' The trapper's reply seemed to come from under Ivanov's elbow, he was so near.

These men were no ordinary hunters, decided Ivanov. The way they covered each other's every move revealed a practised skill at stalking human prey. And they were out to kill him. If he'd been the dummy he'd be lying dead now with a gaping hole in the small of his back. There'd been no warning shot, no attempt at winging him so that they could take him prisoner. They were intent on murder.

Up to then the thought of having to kill these men had bothered Ivanov. Killing was foreign to his nature; even killing for food had at first repelled him. But the bullet which felled the dummy had cleared his mind of scruples; its chill message had been: kill or be killed. No maiming arrow in thigh or arm would help him now; he must aim for eye or throat or heart.

But when was he going to get a chance of taking a shot at them? Though they didn't know it, they'd effectively pinned him down. All he could do was remain as quiet as a mouse and hope that one or the other, when not covered by his companion, would move into his narrow field of fire. But there was little hope they'd oblige him; they were too wary to go anywhere near the dummy.

At last they moved. 'Start quartering, d'you read me?' The sharp command came from Fancy Jacket and when the trapper replied, 'I read you,' Ivanov sensed rather than heard him shifting position. He risked a half turn and caught a glimpse of the trapper's calf-length boots as he slid swiftly and silently through the underbrush, heading away from Ivanov.

Ivanov breathed his relief, then cautiously he pulled aside fronds of bramble to his left and right; it was imperative he widened his field of fire.

When he judged he could swing his bow through an arc of at least ninety degrees he sat back on his haunches and tried to relax. He needed a split second advantage for his arrow to beat Fancy Jacket's buckshot. If he was tensed up he'd be too slow; he must allow his reflexes to take over.

Ivanov caught a snatch of laboured breathing coming from a thicket of birch only twenty feet away and then Fancy Jacket appeared, crawling in the approved military fashion, his shotgun held steady in both hands, his elbows and splayed knees doing all the work.

He hugged the ground so closely that Ivanov despaired of getting in a killing shot. His arrow would be deflected by the clutter of debris on the forest floor.

At that moment a movement to his right caught Ivanov's eye. It was a squirrel scurrying along a slender branch which bent under its weight.

Just a split-second glance was enough for Ivanov. He knew that when the squirrel leapt there'd be a swishing sound as the branch sprang back into place.

The squirrel leapt and Fancy Jacket swung round, looking up and baring his throat for a fleeting moment. It was more than enough time for Ivanov. His arrow caught Fancy Jacket on the Adam's apple, tearing through the cartilage and slewing sideways, the barbed head thrusting deep into his throat and bursting out again to protrude obscenely below his left ear.

Fancy Jacket gave a strangled gurgle, raised his hands to claw at the arrow, then fell onto his side and lay still.

32

Ivanov fitted his second arrow to the bow with trembling hands. His mouth was dry and he swallowed convulsively, fighting an urge to vomit. He couldn't bring himself to look at Fancy Jacket and for a moment he closed his eyes hoping that when he opened them the man would have gone, that what had happened was just a nightmare.

He thought of shouting to the trapper to warn him his companion was dead. That might frighten him away. He didn't want to kill again – never again like that. The look of surprised horror on Fancy Jacket's face would haunt him; it was the look of a child seeing a bogeyman come true.

Then he heard the trapper. He was calling softly and urgently – 'Are you with me, colonel, are you with me? I can't read you.' There was silence, then the voice came again, this time much nearer. 'Pyotr Gavrilovitch, answer me, are you there?'

A rustling of foliage to Ivanov's left heralded the trapper's arrival. He was breathing hard and stood half crouched under the branches of a stunted pine. When he saw Fancy Jacket he gave a low moan and flung himself to the ground, wriggling swiftly to the side of the dead man.

'Pyotr Gavrilovitch!' Dropping his rifle he made as if to raise Fancy Jacket by the shoulders and then saw the arrow. He leapt back and whirled round on his knees, looking fearfully to each side and then up into the trees.

Ivanov could see his eyes staring wild and unfocussed. He was almost blind with panic.

'Don't, please don't!' the trapper suddenly screamed,

and he began to pivot on his bended knees, turning in a tight circle, his arms raised imploringly.

Ivanov gaped. His arrow had turned this bold ruffian into a craven idiot. The man had been brave enough hunting down an escaped prisoner who might, for all he knew, have been armed with shotgun or rifle. But when confronted with the silent, stealthy death dispensed by a primitive weapon he fell to pieces.

'I surrender, I surrender!' he jabbered on, 'look, no gun, no gun!' His rifle lay where he'd dropped it beside Fancy Jacket.

Ivanov wondered what to do. There was no point in taking the man prisoner. In any case he didn't want the trapper to see him and then be able to describe him later.

'Run!' he shouted.

At the sound of Ivanov's voice the man clasped his hands in front of him in an attitude of prayer. He was just too frightened to take in what Ivanov had shouted.

'Run – run for your life!' Ivanov shouted again, and this time to spell out the message he sent an arrow twanging into the branch of a tree a foot above the trapper's head.

'Ayee!' he wailed, and scrambling to his feet began running blindly through the trees. Long after he'd gone, Ivanov could follow his hectic flight by the sound of crashing underbrush and the cries of startled crows bursting out of the woods and flying high in the man's wake. He was one hunter who would never hunt man again.

Part Five

THE KEY TO FREEDOM

33

Ivanov's first thought was to put as great a distance as possible between himself and the still figure of Fancy Jacket, which seemed to lie there reproachfully, reminding him he was the better hunter – and the more deadly killer. It was something many men would have been proud of, but all he wanted to do was get away and forget it ever happened.

But commonsense told him he must try and extract some advantage from the sorry affair. At least he should search the body; Fancy Jacket's papers might tell him a lot.

An army identity card stated he was Pyotr Gavrilovitch Shelestov, aged 42 and born at Kharkov, a colonel of infantry stationed at Ignayetsk where he commanded Military Zone 520. Ivanov hadn't heard of Ignayetsk before and guessed it must be one of the new towns or industrial complexes which were springing up in all parts of Siberia, even in the remotest corners of the taiga.

An unfinished letter he found in Fancy Jacket's back trouser pocket was more helpful. It began, 'Dear Mother,' and was typical of a middle-aged son's letter to an elderly parent – affectionately chatty and reassuring. It filled Ivanov with remorse; instead of that warmly worded letter the old woman would now be getting an official telegram informing her regretfully but coldly that her son was dead.

'I'm settling down nicely at Ignayetsk,' Colonel Shelestov had written, 'and though we're still short on creature comforts it's amazing what has already been done, especially when you remember that only a few months ago there was just nothing here except the endless forest. I've managed to get quite decent barracks put up for my men and they're tremendously pleased with the special rations I mentioned in my previous letter. We might be way out in the back of beyond, but they do feed us well – like princes!

'You remember Sergeant Korbut? He called on us when I was last on leave – an excellent fellow. Well, he's turned out to be a first class woodsman. He can track down game, lay snares, knows where to fish – just as if he'd been born out here. We go hunting together, to a place about twelve miles from here by river where the taiga seems to be teeming with deer....'

Ivanov stopped reading. So they'd arrived by river and Ignayetsk was only twelve miles away. That meant they'd be sending out a party to get the body as soon as the trapper – or Sergeant Korbut it must have been – arrived back.

He must get moving, and his first task must be to find the river – so that he could avoid it. He didn't doubt the sergeant's panic trail through the woods would lead him there, but before setting out he had a thoroughly unpleasant job to do; that was to remove the arrow from Colonel Shelestov's throat.

Ivanov didn't need the arrow – he could easily make another to replace it – but he didn't want to leave any trace of himself behind. When the men from Ignayetsk arrived they'd find Shelestov lying dead with his throat ripped open – a jagged, irregular wound which could not have been caused by knife or bullet. But they'd realise it certainly could have been caused by the claws of bear or wolverine.

Beside the body, untouched, would be Shelestov's shotgun and Korbut's rifle. There'd be no corpse of wolf cub – Ivanov intended burying So-so – and no trace of where he'd camped, for he'd even brush out the trampled grass.

Poor Korbut! Who would believe him when he said that Colonel Shelestov had been killed by an arrow from the bow of a wild man of the woods who kept a young wolf as a pet? It was too tall a story. They'd commiserate with the sergeant and decide that the shock of finding his colonel mortally felled by a bear had been too much for him. Even Korbut, who had not caught so much as a fleeting glimpse of Ivanov, would himself in time come to wonder what had actually happened.

When Ivanov reached the river he wasn't surprised he'd failed to see it when he'd climbed trees earlier that day to study the land ahead. It ran between deep banks, a narrow, fast flowing stream. It didn't seem navigable to Ivanov, but near where Korbut's trail broke out of the woods he found slide marks in the mud at the river's edge. A flat-bottomed rowboat had been hauled ashore and then launched again.

Rowing downstream in that fast current would take the sergeant to Ignayetsk in no time, reflected Ivanov. He had to get clear of the area as quickly as he could, for there was no knowing what speedy transport the army might have at Ignayetsk – motorboats for sure, and more than likely helicopters as well.

Ivanov's original intention had been to keep well away from the river, but now that he'd found where Korbut and Shelestov had landed he felt safe following it upstream. It might give him some good fishing.

He kept as close to the river bank as he could, for fewer trees grew there and this made easier going with the weighty drag pole. By late afternoon he'd covered six miles or more and had settled into a steady, rhythmic plodding when a rumbling noise which he first thought was thunder brought him to a halt.

Then he dived for cover. What he'd heard was a machine of some sort – but not just one; dozens were clattering away in the woods ahead of him. He listened carefully and beneath the racket he detected the steady throb of diesel engines. They were bulldozers – a battery of them – clearing the bush. He'd almost walked into Ignayetsk!

Ivanov cursed himself for his folly in assuming that the town lay down river. Shelestov's letter to his mother had said 'twelve miles by river' and Ivanov had imagined the colonel and his sergeant setting out from Ignayetsk and travelling *up* river in order to reach a part of the taiga still undisturbed and which 'teemed with deer'. It was a natural enough error, but what was he to do now?

Ivanov judged the bulldozers to be half a mile away. Since he'd come this far shouldn't he go on and have a look around? He might learn something which would help him solve the problem of getting home. But first he must hide his drag pole.

A mile back Ivanov had jumped a stream which joined the river and he now retraced his steps and followed the stream deep into the woods. He stopped when he came to a giant spruce growing at the edge of the stream. The water had scoured out a hollow beneath its roots and into this he thrust his drag pole.

He then undressed and wrapped his prison vest, underpants and shirt in Petrisky's hunting jacket. His trousers were so covered in patches of squirrel and hare skins that they were unrecognisable as prison issue. From wolverine waistcoat to moccasins he was now in effect clad entirely in fur and rawhide.

After some thought he put his bow and quiver of

arrows in the hollow as well. He knew he could never bring himself to kill a man again, so there was no point in going armed. He slung the satchel he'd made from rawhide over his shoulder and packed away in it a supply of meat faggots, a coil of snare wire complete with pegs, and a fishing line and hooks. He wanted to be able to cope should he be delayed in getting back to the drag pole.

He was about to set off when for a reason he was unable to fathom he suddenly thought of Sergeant Jablonsky's movement order which he'd left in the pocket of Petrisky's hunting jacket. He was startled; it was as though he'd remembered just in the nick of time something his very life depended on.

He had to smile. That movement order had become a talisman; without it he felt unprotected and unprepared. He was still convinced that a simple ruse involving his identity was the key to his deliverance. And the movement order was the lock which the key would turn.

He groped for the bundle of clothing in the hollow and when he'd extracted the movement order he smoothed it out and re-read it for the thousandth time. He might only be indulging a whim, but he couldn't deny that having the scrap of paper tucked away in his belt eased his mind.

34

Ivanov gave the woods where the bulldozers were working a wide berth and made for the rising land to the south. This enabled him to look down on Ignayetsk when he broke clear of the forest.

The size of the settlement surprised him. He counted more than 200 wooden houses laid out in three rows and converging on a square bounded by large and taller buildings – obviously the stores and administrative offices.

A pontoon bridge spanned the river and led on to an airstrip which ran due west into the taiga. The runway was of concrete and long enough to take the heaviest transports. Also across the river were three sawmills, a cement factory and what looked to Ivanov like the winding gear and outbuildings of a mine.

From where he crouched at the edge of the forest a wide sweep of cleared land sloped gently down to the town. It must have been ploughed and seeded by hands expert in the daunting task of cultivating the taiga soil, for now the entire slope was covered in a lush growth of bluish-green grass. Whoever planned the clearance had an eye for landscape, decided Ivanov, for some handsomely proportioned pines and firs had been left standing at key points on the slope. He could easily imagine he was looking at parkland back home near the Don.

Scarcely a hundred yards from Ivanov a white haired man was forking freshly cut grass into a silage bin, whistling as he worked, while lower down the slope a noisy group followed a winding path which led up into the woods. It was a picnic party.

A man in his early thirties, short but powerfully built, led the way. He was balancing a square wicker-work basket on his left shoulder and tucked under his right arm was a folding canvas chair. Behind him were two women, one much older than the other, while alongside three children chased a football across the grass, shouting excitedly.

'Keep to the path!' the old man working the silage yelled at the children as they drew level with him, but there was no real threat in his voice and when their ball rolled his way he gave it a vigorous kick across uncut grass.

'You'll make the Moscow Dynamos yet!' shouted the man with the basket, and when he reached the silage bin he allowed the women to go ahead and then stealthily produced a bottle from the inside pocket of his jacket and offered it to the old man.

Ivanov watched fascinated. It seemed a century since he'd last seen people behaving like this – relaxed and amiable, not a worry in the world. And he couldn't keep his eyes off the children. They were two girls, aged ten and twelve he guessed, and a small boy not much older than his own Alyosha. The children already had their father's sturdy build and their manner was bold and self-confident. Not for them the anguish of having their father taken away from them in the dead of night, reflected Ivanov bitterly. No dread knocking on the door would ever disturb their dreams.

With a start Ivanov realised the path the children were following led into the forest only some yards from him. He backed away into a thicket of birch, but he needn't have bothered. The picnic party made straight for a little clearing where the man and his wife unpacked the basket while the older woman sat in the canvas chair, her eyes closed, her head back so she could feel the gentle warmth of the early evening sun on her face.

With food on the way the children were quieter now and sat at the old woman's feet, watching their father make a fire. He handed the elder girl a kettle and she tripped off into the woods, singing snatches of a song which tore at Ivanov's heart. It was a Don song – Katerina's favourite.

He sank to the ground where he crouched and buried his face in his hands. He was too miserable to watch any more; he must get away from this happy family, back into the depths of the taiga where there was nothing to remind him of home – at least, nothing so warm and vivid as this.

He raised his head and found the little boy a few feet

away, looking at him gravely and munching away at a thick slab of bread which he held in both hands.

'Daddy,' he called, 'I've found a funny looking man. Come and see. I think he's crying.'

His father grunted and continued sipping at a mug of hot tea without looking up. The boy didn't seem afraid, not even startled. With his father so near no scarecrow of a man lurking in the underbrush was going to frighten him!

Ivanov smiled and the boy smiled back, dropping his bread as he bent to hold out his hand. 'Come!' he said peremptorily, as though talking to a dog, 'Come, come, come!'

Ivanov took his hand and together they stepped out of the thicket of birch into the clearing. The women shrieked and the two girls clung to the old woman's legs. The man dropped his mug of tea and jumped to his feet, looking around him desperately for something he could use as a weapon. He snatched up the kettle and waved it menacingly, hot water splashing from the spout.

Ivanov raised his free hand. 'Please don't be alarmed,' he began, 'I mean no harm—'

'I'm not alarmed,' broke in the man stoutly. He'd gone deathly pale but his voice was firm and he put down the kettle. 'Who are you and what d'you want?'

'I ... I don't know,' stammered Ivanov, looking helplessly from the man to the two women.

'What d'you mean?' the old woman asked sternly but not unkindly. 'D'you mean you don't know what you want or you don't know who you are?'

He didn't answer. The old woman's question had exploded in his mind. Here was the key to his deliverance, the solution to his problem of identity. No wonder he'd felt it staring him in the face; it was so simple.

'I don't know who I am,' he whispered, bowing his head, ashamed at having to deceive these simple people.

'I've no idea who I am or what I'm doing here. Please help me.'

The younger woman was at his side, gripping his arm and pulling him to the fire. 'Poor man, you must be starving,' she said, 'come and eat something. We'll help you.' She turned to her husband. 'We'll help him, won't we Anton?'

The man grinned sheepishly. 'I've got to admit you did scare me for a moment,' he said, 'but you should see yourself – you look like nothing on earth. Come and eat.'

They sat him on a log beside the old woman who poured him a mugful of hot, sweet tea. It was like nectar to Ivanov and he gulped it down, realising only now how his body had been screaming out for sugar.

They offered him bread, sausages, cucumber, apple tart and cakes, but he ate sparingly, explaining that after what he'd had to live on their fare was too rich and would upset him. Even the little he ate dazed him and he found himself engulfed by a desire to sleep. But it didn't worry him; he could afford to relax now. He'd found the key to freedom....

He must have dozed off, for the man gave a sudden cry and gripped him firmly by the arm to stop him tumbling off the log. They'd been watching him in silence, studying his face intently as he ate, the children shyly taking turns to touch and smooth his wolverine waistcoat. Now they all started talking at once.

'We must get him to a doctor,' said the young woman.

'No, a hot bath and a good night's sleep is what he wants,' said the old woman.

'But he's ill,' said Anton. 'Look at his face, have you ever seen anybody look so tired?'

'Bed, bed for sleepy head!' chorused the girls while the little boy shouted shrilly – 'I found him, I found him!'

35

They took him back to Ignayetsk with them, Anton
insisting on having Ivanov's arm round his shoulder to
support him. The children ran ahead screaming excitedly
and when they arrived at the end of the little town's
longest street people left their houses to crowd round and
Anton had to shout at them to clear the way.

A burly mechanic smelling of diesel oil took Ivanov's
other arm and thus they arrived at the medical centre in
the town square, Ivanov supported between the two men
and feeling a dreadful fraud. But he realised his arrival in
Ignayetsk could not have been better arranged had it
been stage managed: it made a classic picture of a man at
the end of his tether being rescued from the taiga.

The doctor at the medical centre was young and
efficient. He listened to Ivanov's chest, palpated his
abdomen, tested his reflexes and took his blood pressure.
Then with an ophthalmoscope he examined Ivanov's eyes
very carefully.

'You can't remember a thing?' he asked.

'No,' said Ivanov, putting panic into his voice, 'I don't
even know who I am. What'll happen to me?'

'Don't worry, your memory will come back. But you
mustn't try too hard to remember – not just yet. What you
need now is plenty of good food and rest.'

The doctor felt Ivanov's scalp and tugged gently at the
remaining hair. 'You've gone bald but your hair is
growing again.' He sounded puzzled. 'When did this
happen?'

'I don't know,' said Ivanov. 'I can remember being ill. I

lay for days in a cave unable to move and when I got better I found my teeth were falling out.'

The doctor examined Ivanov's mouth. 'No sign of scurvy.' He was frankly puzzled now. 'You'll have to tell me everything you can remember about your illness. But not now – I'll do a blood test first.'

Ivanov didn't have to pretend to be concerned. 'Then there's something seriously wrong with me?'

'No – at least, not now. In fact, you're astonishingly fit for somebody rescued from the taiga. But I'd like to know what that illness was....' The doctor fell silent and pulled thoughtfully at his underlip, not taking his eyes off Ivanov. 'But what puzzles me even more is your amnesia,' he added quietly.

'Oh,' said Ivanov, suddenly alarmed.

'I thought it might be concussion,' went on the doctor, 'but I had a good look at your eyes and there's no sign of your having had a knock on the head. We'll do an encephalogram – an x-ray on your brain – to make sure there's no damage but I'm already fairly convinced the cause is nothing physical – more likely an emotional tie-up of some sort.'

Ivanov took a deep breath. This doctor was too conscientious for his liking; it wasn't going to be easy fooling him.

'Don't look so worried!' The doctor was smiling at him now. 'You're all tensed up like an over-wound watch. That won't help you get your memory back, so unwind, relax. I'm going to put you to bed for a few days and all I want you to do is eat and sleep and not think about anything. Nobody's going to bother you, I'll see to that.'

The doctor was as good as his word. For two days Ivanov lay in bed in a little room at the back of the medical centre, away from the bustle of the emergency ward and his only visitors were the doctor and a nurse.

His food was brought to him by the nurse, a tall, gaunt woman from the Ukraine who never smiled and stood over him as he ate, waiting silently until he had cleared his plate. For Ivanov's starved tastebuds the food was a daily voyage of discovery. Even plain bread had a flavour he'd never noticed before. 'You feed me like a prince,' he told the sad nurse, then remembered that Colonel Shelestov had used this exact phrase in his letter to his mother.

That set him wondering how long the Ignayetsk police would take to suspect him of being concerned in the colonel's death. They were bound to link Sergeant Korbut's breathless story about a wild man of the woods with his own dramatic deliverance from the taiga. By now the colonel's body would have been recovered and he must expect at any moment a visit from the police. He'd have to brace himself for some tough questioning.

But that was an ordeal he felt he could cope with, for he'd used his time in bed to prepare a plausible account of his life in the taiga. What worried him was how to maintain his pretence of amnesia.

He'd counted on the doctor being like the bullying and bungling medical misfits employed in the prison camps; instead he was a conscientious and competent man whose lively sympathy for his patients made him dangerously observant. If he failed to convince the doctor he'd lost his memory his bid for freedom would founder before it had properly started.

Ever since the old woman's question in the woods had inspired the idea of amnesia Ivanov had been turning it over in his mind and he had now completely convinced himself that it was the only ruse which could lead him to liberty.

Previously he'd been led astray by the question of identity, futilely racking his brains for a way of tricking the authorities into believing he was somebody else. His mistake had been to place the onus of proof upon himself.

Now, by pretending not to know who he was, he'd shifted the onus of proof on to the authorities.

Ivanov turned over in his comfortable bed and whispered to the empty room: 'It's so simple and yet foolproof. Instead of me telling them who I am, they'll have to tell me!'

And who would they tell him he was? Ivanov permitted himself a sly grin. This was where Sergeant Jablonsky's movement order came in. They'd find it in his belt and off they'd scamper on a false scent which would take them so far from the real Ivan Mikailovitch Ivanov that they'd never find their way back.

Of course their records might prove positively he wasn't Jablonsky, but how then did he come by the sergeant's movement order? That proved he had something to do with the crashed plane. Was he, then, one of the aircrew or a security guard? They had twelve men to choose from.

Ivanov now sat up in bed, too excited to lie still. He knew he was not just guessing what the authorities would do; he was predicting their every move, for they'd be working within a scenario he'd prepared for them.

But what if they behaved illogically and ignored Sergeant Jablonsky's movement order? In that case his illness would be the clincher. Already the young doctor had been alerted by his symptoms and when the experts were called in they'd find positive proof that he'd been poisoned by the abominable chemical the plane had been carrying.

'They can get as suspicious as they like,' Ivanov whispered jubilantly, 'but my illness will stop them in their tracks. It's a provable fact which ties me fast to that plane and its confounded cargo.'

What would they then do? They couldn't just choose any identity for him from among the thirteen men on board the plane, for there were relatives to be considered.

Ivanov tried to put himself into the bureaucratic mind. They liked having everything neatly labelled, he told himself, and they'd positively resent having on their hands a citizen with no name....

He felt his face flushing with triumph. Their very nature would impel them into giving him a brand new identity. He'd leave them a new man and a free man – with a police record as clean as the taiga snow!

36

But first, Ivanov reminded himself – and it was a sobering thought – he had to pull the wool over the eyes of the young doctor. Doyarenko was his name, a Ukrainian like the nurse. He'd volunteered for work in Siberia because of the clinical experience it would give him.

'I've had to cope with just about every condition in the medical textbooks,' he cheerfully told Ivanov. 'Take your amnesia, for instance. I've never come across a case before but I've been reading it up, so don't worry, between us we'll beat it.'

Ivanov groaned to himself and desperately tried to remember all he knew about amnesia, which was precious little. If only he could somehow snatch a quick look at Doyarenko's textbooks.

But the need didn't arise. On the third day of his stay at the medical centre a crestfallen Doyarenko ushered in two uniformed men – one an army captain and the other a police lieutenant.

'I'm going to lose you,' announced the doctor, genuine regret in his voice, 'I was so looking forward to helping you. But Captain Rodichev will explain.'

The army captain smiled at Ivanov and gave a little

apologetic shrug. 'Sorry to make you leave this comfortable billet so soon,' he said, 'but I've had instructions to get you to Omsk without delay. The doctor here tells me you're fit to travel.'

Ivanov had to suppress a surge of glee. They'd found Sergeant Jablonsky's movement order and taken the bait.

As if to confirm it Captain Rodichev fumbled in his tunic pocket and produced an envelope from which he carefully extracted the flimsy scrap of paper which Ivanov had come to regard as his passport to freedom.

'Please be careful how you handle it,' said Rodichev, 'it's pretty tattered. I want you to read it and tell me if it rings a bell.'

Ivanov took his time, silently mouthing the words of the movement order as he read it, then turning it over to look at the back, as though hoping to find enlightenment there. 'Is this mine?' he asked.

'Never mind that!' said the police lieutenant roughly, 'just tell us, are you or aren't you Jablonsky?'

Before Ivanov could reply Doyarenko cut in with a contemptuous snort. 'If you want this man's memory to seize up for ever that's just the way to set about it!'

Captain Rodichev gestured soothingly with both hands. 'Easy, doc, nobody's going to bully your patient.' He glared at the lieutenant and then turned to Ivanov. 'To answer your question, we found the movement order tucked away in a slit in your belt, so naturally we've assumed it's yours. Doesn't the name Jablonsky mean anything to you?'

Ivanov looked again at the movement order and slowly shook his head, the perfect picture of a puzzled and confused man trying his best to be helpful. He made to hand the scrap of paper back to the captain, then stopped and looked at it yet again. 'What's this schedule X Z cargo I was supposed to guard?' he asked with wide-eyed innocence.

The policeman shifted uncomfortably in his chair. He was beetle-browed and his shifty, black-button eyes almost disappeared when he frowned. 'I told you not to show it to him,' he hissed at the captain.

'Cargo?' said Doyarenko, reaching for the movement order. 'A special cargo, eh? Would it by any chance have been a chemical of some sort?'

The police lieutenant grunted impatiently. 'Why d'you ask?'

'For a damn good reason!' The young doctor was fast losing his patience with the policeman. 'You should have told me about this. It could explain a lot about this man's condition.'

'I don't follow,' said Captain Rodichev, 'unless you mean his amnesia was caused by–'

'I'm not referring to that,' interrupted Doyarenko impatiently. He had turned to Ivanov. 'You've been exposed to a toxic gas of some sort. I knew it right from the start, but I couldn't believe it – not out in the unpolluted taiga. Impossible! But this plane and its cargo, it explains–'

'Doctor.' The police lieutenant had sprung to his feet. 'It's not for us to explain anything to this man!'

Doyarenko looked at him coldly. 'Perhaps not for you. He isn't your patient.'

He turned back to Ivanov. 'Your symptoms just shouted at me – the vomiting, the delirium, the loss of hair and teeth and' – the doctor bent over Ivanov and touched the back of both his hands – 'something you yourself didn't notice at the time, blisters on your hands and arms and face. The scars are still there.'

Ivanov looked at his hands and pulled up the sleeves of his pyjamas. The doctor was right. 'How could I have missed seeing them?' he asked helplessly.

'Because you weren't looking for them – and I was. But don't worry, the scars will disappear.'

'That's not what I'm worrying about,' said Ivanov, 'what–'

'I know,' broke in Doyarenko, 'what you want to know is what damage has been done. I'll be frank, your blood tests show a marked drop in lymphocytes – the white blood cells which fight disease. But I'm sure that's on the mend because you seem to have rid your system of the poison. Your hair is growing again and what teeth you've got left are soundly rooted.'

'No lasting effects, then?' said Ivanov, visibly relieved.

'None at all so far as I can see. But to be on the safe side I'll be writing a report for the people in Omsk so that they can take more blood tests and keep you under observation for a while.' Doyarenko turned to Captain Rodichev. 'Make sure you show them that movement order. They'll check back on it and find out what chemical the plane was carrying. That'll help them no end.'

Captain Rodichev nodded and then looked questioningly at the police lieutenant who had his back half turned to Doyarenko as though to dissociate himself from the doctor's friendly exchange with Ivanov.

'If you're quite sure you've finished,' the lieutenant said in a heavy attempt at sarcasm, 'I should like to put a few questions on another matter.'

'Go ahead,' said Rodichev, adding for Doyarenko's benefit – 'it's to do with poor Shelestov.' Ivanov silently thanked the captain for warning him of the switch in topic. He'd been so engrossed in what the doctor had to say that he'd completely forgotten the dead colonel.

'What did you live on in the taiga?' asked the policeman.

'Nuts, berries, hare and suslik. I also did some fishing.'

'How'd you catch the hares?'

'Snared them with wire.'

'Where'd you get the wire?'

'Shortly after my illness I came across an abandoned camp. I grubbed round for anything I could use. As well as the wire for snaring I found a short length of thicker wire which I made into fish hooks.'

'You didn't make a bow?'

'What d'you mean, a bow?'

'A bow and arrow.'

Ivanov shook his head and gave the policeman a wry grin. 'You don't muck around with tomfool ideas like that when you're starving.'

The policeman grunted. Whether he agreed or not it was difficult to tell. 'Did you ever come across anybody armed with a bow?'

'I met nobody until I was found by Anton and his family.'

'And it's true they found you cowering under a bush?'

'Yes,' Ivanov looked down, avoiding the eyes fixed on him. 'I was afraid,' he mumbled.

'Afraid? Afraid of what?' snapped the lieutenant.

'Afraid that what I was seeing wasn't real.'

'You mean,' put in Doyarenko gently, 'that you'd been imagining seeing people?'

'Yes,' whispered Ivanov, 'once I saw a group of women beating their washing on the stones beside a river, but when I ran up to them, shouting and weeping for joy, they just disappeared into thin air.'

'Uh, uh!' The doctor clucked his sympathy. 'That's a typical hallucination – a classical one in fact. You're lonely and afraid so you see something homely and comforting and then – eureka! – it's gone.'

'And what happens when at last you do meet somebody who turns out to be real?' asked Rodichev with a sly look at the police lieutenant, 'd'you kill him?'

Doyarenko snorted and both he and Rodichev burst out laughing.

119

'That's not fair!' the lieutenant protested, 'I don't suspect this man, not for a moment, but I had to follow up on Korbut's story, I had no choice.'

'And a fine story it was!' spluttered the doctor, 'a killer terrorising the taiga with a bow—'

'And a tame wolf!' exclaimed Rodichev.

'Poor Korbut!' The doctor stopped laughing. 'He's worse off than our friend here. And as for Shelestov' – he shrugged sadly – 'I've never seen an arrow wound, but I've seen what bears can do....'

Ivanov looked from face to face and read in each a plain disbelief that he, the gentle wanderer come in from the taiga, could conceivably have killed Colonel Shelestov.

But he didn't exult. It had all been too easy: first, their unquestioning assumption that Jablonsky's movement order was his; then the doctor linking his illness with the chemical on the plane; and now the assurance that nobody suspected him of being Korbut's wild man.

It was too good to be true. There must be a fly in the ointment, thought Ivanov, a setback or a hazard he hadn't taken into account.

And he was right. 'By the way,' said the police lieutenant to Doyarenko as he and Rodichev rose to leave, 'I'll be sending a man along to take his fingerprints.'

Fingerprints! The shock was almost too much for Ivanov. His heart gave a lurch and his vision blurred. How could he have overlooked such an obvious and unerring pointer to his identity! His illness must have affected his mind, for in all the time he'd spent working out a way to hoodwink the authorities he'd forgotten they held that trump card. He'd been obsessed with his changed appearance – cock-a-hoop because he no longer looked like his photographs in the official records. But his fingerprints were with his records and they remained nchanged. It was now only a matter of days before they ound out who he was. Ivanov felt himself spinning iddily in a vortex of despair.

'Eh! Take it easy now, take it easy!' It was Doyarenko peaking and he moved swiftly over to Ivanov, sitting on he edge of the bed to take his pulse. 'You look done in. This little session's been too much for you.'

Rodichev and the police lieutenant had stopped in the oorway. 'Is he all right?' asked Rodichev anxiously.

'Yes,' said the doctor, 'just a dizzy spell. We can expect hat after what he's been through. Who'll be dealing with im in Omsk?'

'The K G B,' said the police lieutenant, adding with relish, he top men want to see him.'

Doyarenko's face fell. 'I can't certify him fit for *them*!' e exclaimed.

'Too late, my dear doctor!' the lieutenant replied, his .erce pig eyes flashing with triumph, 'you've cleared him or travel. He's their patient now!'

Part Six

THE LIONS' DEN

37

Vassily Andreyevitch Khustov tried to look stern, a
befitted a lieutenant in the KGB. But though h
frowned as he arranged the papers on his desk and thoug
he set his mouth into a thin, straight line, he fooled
nobody – least of all his clerk, who stood stiffly to attentio
before him.

The plain fact is that Khustov was by nature an amiable
soul and this was positively telegraphed in the frank gaz
of his blue eyes and in his ready smile which even now
with lips pressed tightly together, lurked at the corners c
his mouth.

'Why the hell does he want it?' he barked at the clerk.

'I don't know, Comrade Lieutenant, he just said h
wanted to see the report and for you to take it to him.
The clerk, grown grey in the service of the security police
had developed a sixth sense for departmental rows. On
was now brewing and he fervently hoped his lieutenan
would emerge unscathed. He liked Khustov because h
was so typical of the new sort of officer being recruited t
the KGB since Stalin's death – honest, uncompli
cated young men as yet uncorrupted by the deviou
careerists who ran the service.

'I wonder what's wrong with it?' Khustov muttered
riffling through the papers of the report. 'But don't stand
there like an idiot – draw up a chair.'

'Vassily Andreyevitch,' the clerk leant forward confidentially, 'I've been chatting up some of the lads over at HQ and I gather it's the cover story that Colonel Leykin is querying. So something must have turned up. And the only thing that could happen to spoil the cover story is for a survivor to appear. I know it's unlikely but–'

'A survivor!' exploded Khustov, 'you must be mad, there couldn't be any survivors, not after all this time, and yet–' He leant back in his chair and grinned suddenly at the clerk, all thought for being sternly businesslike quickly forgotten. 'You know, Voloshin, I've said it before and I'll say it again, you're a genius. You've put your finger on the only reason the report could be queried at this late stage.'

'Thank you, Vassily Andreyevitch,' said Voloshin humbly, 'you're too kind. But may I go further and suggest that being forewarned is to be forearmed....?'

Khustov tried to frown again. 'It's my report so I carry the can. I hope you're not suggesting I shift the blame?'

'Not for a moment, Comrade Lieutenant, but others had a hand in that report. Take the medical side, for instance. You might well think that Captain Brednikov should be alerted so that he'll be ready to see the colonel as well.'

Khustov shuffled the sheets in front of him. 'Ah, here's the medical report. Brednikov says that any survivors would be so badly contaminated they could not possibly live for more than nine months to a year. How long is it now since the plane disappeared?'

'More than two years.'

Khustov sighed. 'Poor old Brednikov, it's he who's carrying the can. My cover story for the relatives was based on his report, it says so here.'

Voloshin sighed as well. 'I'm afraid our medical officer is always too precise, he should hedge his bets....'

The clerk was right as usual, thought Khustov glumly.

Brednikov was that sort of man – a dogmatic, fussy army doctor of the old school. He should have been more vague, particularly as he knew practically nothing about the chemical the plane was carrying.

Strong-nerved as Khustov was he couldn't help an involuntary shudder at the thought of the drubbing the old doctor would get from Colonel Leykin – if indeed a survivor had turned up.

'You'd better warn Captain Brednikov to stand by for the fireworks,' he told Voloshin, 'and tell him to mug up on that chemical the plane was carrying – tetra something or other.'

'Tetrachlorodioxin,' said the clerk, 'or TCDD for short.'

That was it – TCDD, thought Khustov as he stepped out smartly across the parade ground to the HQ hutments. They'd been told TCDD was the latest type of defoliant – guaranteed by the boffins to kill all types of vegetation from the algae in pond scum to the giant firs of the taiga. Khustov grimaced. This wasn't his idea of how wars should be fought but he couldn't avoid becoming involved when the KGB section he commanded was detailed to provide security for a shipment of TCDD being sent by air from the Chemical Warfare Centre at Omsk to a remote corner of the Siberian Far East where it was to be tested.

The plane had never arrived at its destination and was presumed to have crashed in the taiga. Though an intensive air search had been mounted, no wreckage was found. After waiting for a year to see if any survivors turned up the KGB had presumed that all on board were dead and Khustov was given the task of preparing a cover story so that the next-of-kin could be informed without revealing to them the true nature of the dead men's last mission.

Khustov groaned aloud. The possibility of there being a

survivor had just not entered into his calculations; his cover story would now be blown apart. Colonel Leykin would not be pleased.

38

But Khustov had a surprise. Colonel Leykin was in the best of spirits, sitting far back in his swivel chair, one leg resting elegantly across the corner of his desk. He was a little man, slim and carefully groomed, with a swarthy face and shiny black hair which didn't show a streak of grey though he was already touching sixty.

'You seem worried, my dear Khustov,' he said amiably. 'Do sit down.'

Khustov smiled uncertainly. 'The Comrade Colonel doesn't send for old reports, filed away some two years ago, just to compliment the author.'

Leykin laughed. 'Nicely put. So? Why have I sent for you?'

'A survivor perhaps?'

Leykin sat up in surprise, taking his leg from off the corner of the desk. 'Good thinking, my lad, you're brighter than I thought.'

Khustov blinked his blue eyes and felt himself blushing. 'I'm afraid I can't take the credit, it was Voloshin, my clerk....'

Leykin jumped to his feet and walked to the window and back, hands to his head, pretending to clutch at his hair in despair. 'Oh, Khustov, poor Khustov,' he moaned theatrically, 'how many times have I told you not to be so frank? That's not the way to get on in this service!'

Khustov shifted uneasily in his chair. Aleksandr Nikolayevitch Leykin was an enigma to him. He was a

martinet, a stickler for the military proprieties who kept
his subordinates at arm's length. And yet he could put on
a performance like this – a sort of pantomime in irony.
Did he really mean the KGB was no place for
men who were frank and honest? Khustov suppressed the
treasonous thought; a more dedicated and efficient officer
than Leykin couldn't be found in the service.

'I'm sorry, it's my nature....' he stammered.

But Leykin had reseated himself and was now glaring
across the desk at Khustov, the pantomime over. 'The
report,' he snapped, holding out a hand.

As the colonel turned the pages of the report he made
notes from it on a memo pad, writing swiftly. Khustov
stole a glance at the bowed head and not for the first time
found himself almost mesmerised by the hideous scar
which ran from under the colonel's sleek hair, across his
left temple and down the side of his face. A war wound,
he had been told; apart from his service in the
KGB the colonel had a distinguished military
record, having commanded a division in the last years of
the war. But since then somewhere along the way he'd
blotted his copybook and – so it was whispered in the
mess – had spent four years in a Siberian labour camp.
Not that the colonel had done anything wrong himself; it
was something to do with his son, one of those writer
fellows, Khustov had heard. The thought disturbed him.
Having the sins of the son visited upon the father wasn't
his idea of Soviet justice.

Leykin's rasping voice broke in on his thoughts. 'Send
for Brednikov. It's that old sawbones I've to take to
pieces, not you.'

'He's waiting outside.'

Leykin looked up from the papers in front of him and
Khustov could have sworn that for a fleeting moment a
mischievous grin creased the grim mouth. 'Again your
clerk's doing?'

Khustov nodded unhappily and rose to fetch Brednikov. He'd rightly anticipated what followed. Leykin paced the room in rapid, heel-tapping strides, snarling all sorts of insults at the old doctor, who stood rigidly to attention, beads of sweat coursing down his florid features.

'Sit down!' Leykin finally snapped, 'and help us sort out this mess.' He turned to Khustov. 'How does a survivor affect the cover story?'

'Blows it apart.'

'So he can't be sent home?'

'If he went home he'd be turning up from the dead. They'd be digging up his coffin to see what's inside.'

'Coffin?' The icy edge had returned to Leykin's voice. 'I think you'd better explain.'

Khustov's heart missed a beat and his face drained of colour as the enormity of the error he'd made hit him. He should have ordered caskets – small ones just big enough to contain a handful of 'remains'. Instead he'd tried to be clever by pretending the bodies had been recovered.

'I sent sealed coffins to the next-of-kin,' he said, his voice not much above a whisper, 'with instructions to the area commanders to give each man a military funeral.'

'Very commendable – the military funeral, I mean, they were all regulars,' Leykin remarked drily, 'but why coffins?'

Khustov shrugged helplessly. 'I felt they deserved a proper send-off and–'

'But what's in them?' interrupted Leykin, 'what in heaven's name did you put in the coffins?'

'Bricks wrapped in paper.'

Leykin glared at him in disbelief. 'Bricks!' was all he could say.

'It's not easy to get corpses,' began Khustov, but a savage grin from Leykin silenced him.

'Don't tell me you actually indented for corpses?'

'I didn't get that far,' said Khustov, adding lamely, 'I tried the city morgue but they told me all the bodies were spoken for.'

'No odd bods, eh?' The colonel made a choking sound and swung round in his swivel chair, turning his back on his subordinates. They exchanged an alarmed glance. Was Khustov's clanger too much for the old boy, had it brought on an apoplectic fit? ... Or was he laughing?

But the colonel had swung round again, his face a mask. 'How many coffins did you send out?'

'Fourteen.'

'All to different places?'

'Yes.'

'So we've fourteen coffins full of bricks buried in fourteen cemeteries scattered all over the country?'

Khustov nodded miserably. What a mess! No survivor could be sent home now, for the relatives would want to know what they'd buried in the local cemetery. Word would get round and coffins full of bricks would be dug up all over Russia! If only he'd admitted no bodies had been recovered there'd be no problem, for caskets could have then been used and people had come to regard the 'ashes' in caskets as symbolic. But bricks in coffins were no symbol; they were a plain fraud.

Leykin must have read his thoughts. 'I can see you realise how stupid you've been, but we've no time for that now, we've got to decide what to do with the survivor. So start thrashing that brain of yours, Khustov. Prove to me it's not packed with bricks like your blasted coffins!'

39

Might I make a suggestion, Comrade Colonel?' It was
Brednikov speaking for the first time. He'd recovered
from the colonel's drubbing and was now his fussy self
again, itching to get a word in.

'Couldn't we have the man detained for medical observation?' he asked eagerly, 'after all, he was in a plane full
of a dangerous chemical, wasn't he?'

'Put him under medical observation for the rest of his
life?' asked Leykin drily.

'Why not?' Brednikov smiled brightly at the colonel.
'There'd be no administrative problem. The boffins at the
Chemical Warfare Department would take him over.
They've no idea yet how that chemical affects humans
and we've got a guinea pig for them. He must be just
about pickled in the stuff.'

Leykin grunted. 'You might have something there,' he
conceded grudgingly, 'what d'you think, Khustov?'

The lieutenant looked upset. 'But not for life. We can't
have a man put away like that when he's done nothing....
In any case, the boffins wouldn't want him that long.'

'There are special hospitals, you know,' put in
Brednikov, and again he smiled brightly at the colonel.
He felt he was winning his way back into Leykin's favour.

'Well, Khustov, what d'you say? It's your pigeon and
I'm leaving you to decide.' Leykin was looking straight
into Khustov's eyes and the lieutenant knew that for once
the colonel wasn't taunting him. His steady gaze held a
challenge – even an invitation – to disagree with the
obsequious old doctor.

'No,' he said firmly, 'we can't do it, we mustn't forget

there's such a thing as due legal process. It's a basic right which all citizens can claim.'

'Since when—?' began Brednikov, but a frown from Leykin silenced him.

'In that case,' went on Leykin remorselessly, 'what d'you suggest, my dear Khustov? What's left for us to do?'

Khustov looked hopelessly from one to the other. 'What about a switch in identity,' he began uncertainly, then warmed to the idea. 'Couldn't we persuade the survivor to become somebody else? Appeal to his patriotism, to his sense of duty – that sort of thing?'

'Rubbish!' sneered Brednikov, 'no man would—'

'Not so fast, Brednikov!' interrupted Leykin, rapping his knuckles impatiently on the desk, 'that's your trouble, jumping to conclusions with only half the facts.' He turned to Khustov. 'And what if I were to tell you that the man doesn't know who he is – he's lost his memory?'

Khustov's blue eyes opened wide. 'That would be splendid, Aleksandr Nikolayevitch! We can give him a completely new identity and then our problem's solved!'

Brednikov frowned. 'Amnesia, eh?' he muttered suspiciously. 'But in that case,' he said to Leykin, 'how do we know he's a survivor from the plane carrying the chemicals?'

Leykin flipped open a drawer in his desk and took out a folder which he handed to Khustov. 'Open that and tell me if you recognise the document inside.'

The lieutenant opened the folder and gasped. 'It's the movement order I made out to Sergeant Jablonsky!' He held up the flimsy scrap of paper between finger and thumb. 'D'you mean the survivor could be Jablonsky?'

'That's for you to find out. All we know is that a few days ago this man turned up at a settlement called Ignayetsk, walking in from the taiga like a bear. They found the movement order tucked away in his belt.'

Leykin turned to Brednikov. 'It seems they've a bright

medical type at Ignayetsk. Off his own bat he found that the man had been chemically poisoned, so there's little doubt he's been contaminated by the cargo on the plane. I want you to get hold of the Omsk people and tell them to send one of their medical experts up here to examine him.'

The colonel dismissed Brednikov with a nod, but when Khustov rose to leave as well he waved him back into his seat. Long after the door had closed on the doctor Leykin remained silent, tapping one finger gently on the desk top, lost in thought.

'Fishy!' he finally exclaimed, 'don't you smell something fishy about this?' He shot a quick glance at Khustov, who stared blankly back.

'No? Well, take the probability factor first. All the odds were against him – the plane crash, contamination from the chemical, starvation, freezing to death – but he survived the lot. Then take the time factor. It's more than two years since the plane crashed, so where's he been? Don't tell me in the taiga for two years – for two Arctic winters without proper shelter and clothing.'

'You mean he's not a survivor – not Jablonsky or any of the other men?'

'I mean he needn't be.' Leykin again looked hard at Khustov. 'Put your mind to his amnesia for a moment. Handy isn't it? And I mean handy for us, in fact, quite wonderfully convenient. It's as though the man knew what we wanted – was providing us with a modus operandi. I've a feeling we're being manipulated....'

This was Leykin at his best, thought Khustov. There was no sharper mind in the KGB when it came to discovering irregularities of any sort. He was constantly on the alert for facts that didn't fit, for hidden motives, for coincidences that were too neat.

'But why should this fellow want to deceive us?' asked Khustov, 'what's in it for him?'

'That's what we've got to work on. He must benefi
somehow, but exactly how baffles me at the moment....'

Leykin stood up abruptly and began pacing the room i
his short, jerky strides, his head bent low. Just like
restless wolf, thought Khustov. He's fastened onto th
scent of something and he won't give up until he's tracked
it down.

'Right!' Leykin barked dismissively. 'Get on with it
Give this man the grilling of life, get right under hi
his skin, turn him inside out – and then I'll have a g
myself.'

40

Ivanov should have been cheered by the room they gave
him. The floor was carpeted, the window curtained, and a
vase of freshly cut flowers stood on his bedside table. Ever
his hospital bed had a homely touch, the drab olive
blankets out of sight under an eiderdown which had a
raised pattern in coloured thread showing a knight i
armour rescuing a lady in distress. In the evenings the
pale autumn sunshine slanted low through the window
casting the pattern in sharp relief, and Ivanov would ther
screw up his eyes and imagine he was with the knight
wandering free in a fairy tale world....

But he couldn't fool himself for long. Any day now –
no, any hour, any minute – he expected a KGB
officer to appear at his bedside and wave the incriminating
fingerprint cards under his nose. The prospect plunged
Ivanov into the deepest gloom.

The doctors doing medical tests on him misinterpreted
his despondency. 'No need to worry,' they told him, 'al
the poison has worked itself out and you're back to

normal.' They must have been instructed to reassure him, for they told him more than he'd ever expected to be told.

'You've had dioxin poisoning – probably the first man in the world to have it,' the head doctor told him, almost admiringly.

'What is it? It sounds awful,' said Ivanov.

'It's an element released in the air when tetra-chlorodioxin has been used – a sort of weedkiller you might say.'

'Just a weedkiller?'

'Well, it was intended as such originally, but it's too powerful, it kills all plant life.'

'What you'd call a defoliant?' asked Ivanov boldly, 'I seem to remember reading somewhere about chemicals being used to strip the countryside of all plant life.'

The doctor hesitated, obviously wondering how far he was allowed to go. 'I suppose you could call it that,' he admitted reluctantly, 'but don't let it bother you. We've done any number of tests and we're certain now you've not suffered any lasting damage.'

'But what about my blood?' asked Ivanov, 'the doctor in Ignayetsk said something about the white cells being affected.'

'All back to normal. We've watched that carefully because leukaemia was a possible complication, but I'm glad to say it hasn't turned out that way. You've got absolutely nothing to worry about.'

Low spirited as he was Ivanov couldn't help feeling elated, and though he reminded himself that being given a clean bill of health only meant he'd manage to survive an extra year or two in his next labour camp, he decided he much preferred to die of malnutrition and overwork than of a sinister man-made disease. And in any case, why should he deny himself the satisfaction of knowing he was fit again? Why not enjoy what time was left to him in the hospital?

It was in this relaxed mood that Ivanov entered into a series of sessions with the psychiatrist investigating his amnesia. Now that the KGB would soon be on to him there was no need any longer to weigh his every word. He wouldn't tell the truth of course, but neither would he worry about being caught out.

Accordingly, Ivanov gave little thought to the questions put to him, speaking freely and seizing on the first answers to spring to mind. Sometimes he elaborated recklessly and watched fascinated as the psychiatrist religiously noted down everything he said, filling sheet after sheet of paper. This had a surprising result.

At the end of his third day examining Ivanov the psychiatrist checked back carefully through his notes, underlining certain passages and writing further notes in the margins. Finally he shuffled the papers into a neat pile which he slapped down sharply on the table in front of him. It was a dismissive gesture; he'd finished with Ivanov.

'Here it comes,' thought Ivanov, 'he's now going to tear me apart for fooling around.'

But the psychiatrist wasn't angry. 'I was warned you might be putting on a bit of an act,' he began quietly, 'and I don't mind admitting you had me wondering at times. But you're not shamming.' He tapped the pile of notes. 'These prove conclusively you're an amnesiac. Everything you've told me fits into a pattern which just can't be fabricated.'

The astonished Ivanov didn't know what to say.

'You've endured a trauma – a shock – of quite cataclysmic proportions,' went on the psychiatrist, 'probably something to do with that plane crash you can't remember. It's basically a form of hysteria and takes some shifting, particularly if as I suspect you're in what we call a state of fugue. It might be weeks, months or even years before you get your memory back.'

Ivanov could only gape. 'It's as bad as that?' he finally

stammered, hoping his astonished silence had been taken for dismay. 'But surely you know who I am,' he added urgently, as though clinging to a last hope, 'at least you can tell me that, can't you?'

It was the psychiatrist's turn to be surprised. 'God no!' he exclaimed. 'If I knew who you were I'd have told you right away. A man's name is a powerful lever. It can rip aside amnesia and bring everything back.'

'But somebody must know,' persisted Ivanov, 'what about the authorities? They've records they can check – identity cards, photographs and....' He hestitated then decided to plunge on. 'Fingerprints. We're all finger-printed, aren't we? They must have my prints somewhere.'

The psychiatrist nodded thoughtfully. 'I suppose so, but nothing's turned up so far. Why not ask Lieutenant Khustov what he's doing about it? He's the man in charge of your case and you'll be seeing him tomorrow.'

'I'll do that,' murmured Ivanov, careful to continue to sound dejected but feeling a fresh spark of hope kindling within him. Had a miracle happened? Had the filing systems been fouled up and his prints lost?

41

But it was no miracle. It was just the creaking machinery of an overloaded bureaucracy taking its time, an indig-nant Lieutenant Khustov explained next day.

'It's not our fault,' he protested, his blue eyes flashing, 'so be patient for a few days more, then we'll know who you are – I'm sure of that.'

He described how the country was split into regions, each having its own civilian records bureau. 'We had to send out more than fifty photographed copies of your fingerprints,' he said, 'and that's not counting the armed forces.'

His face creased into a cheerful grin. 'One thing though we already know – you're no criminal.'

Ivanov looked up startled. He'd been allowed to leave the hospital that morning and was now seated in Khustov's office, facing the lieutenant across a desk. 'I'm no criminal?' he asked uncertainly.

'You seem disappointed,' laughed Khustov, 'but you've no lurid past, I'm afraid, no criminal dossier.'

'At least the police wasted no time,' said Ivanov, but he didn't listen as Khustov launched into a paean of praise for the police records system, which was highly central-ised and computer-operated. He was instead trying to work out why he wasn't in the police files.

Then it occurred to him that of course he was a *political* offender and the authorities insisted on distinguishing between political and criminal offenders at all levels. In which case his dossier must be with the KGB. There was no need for them to look for it; they already had it in their own records office! And yet Khustov hadn't said anything about KGB records. Was it a trick? Or hadn't Khustov thought of checking his own files?

Ivanov had to suppress a chuckle. What he'd predicted was happening: the KGB were being led astray by Sergeant Jablonsky's movement order. They were so concerned over Ivanov's link with the crashed plane, so intent on establishing his identity through the routine channels of civilian, military and police records that it hadn't crossed their minds that he might already be in their own files – that he was in fact their prisoner!

But it wouldn't be long before the penny dropped, thought Ivanov, and then poor Khustov would get it in the neck.

The young lieutenant had been another surprise for Ivanov; he could hardly believe that this amiable young man, so frank and obviously honest, was a KGB officer. Of course he could be what was known as a 'softener' – the interrogator who wins the suspect's confidence by befriending and then pretending to shield him him from the rough treatment threatened by others.

It was an age-old ploy and Ivanov had already caught a glimpse of one of the grimmer of Khustov's colleagues – a full colonel, his face hatchet thin and swarthy, with a livid scar running from hairline to chin. An ugly customer. No doubt the kindly Khustov would do his damnedest to save him from that man's clutches!

All that morning and late into the afternoon Khustov questioned Ivanov. They were poring over maps, with Ivanov pretending to try his best to trace his wanderings in the taiga, when the door opened and the colonel with the scar walked to the back of the room and stood there without saying a word.

Ivanov could feel the man's eyes boring into the back of his neck and he looked inquiringly at Khustov, who avoided the glance and fumbled distractedly with his maps, dropping one to the floor. The young lieutenant was suddenly very nervous.

'I don't think I've had the pleasure,' said Ivanov, swinging round in his chair. The colonel clicked his heels and nodded stiffly. 'I didn't want to disturb you,' he said.

Khustov sprang to his feet, almost knocking the table over. 'This is our commanding officer,' he said eagerly, 'Colonel Leykin.'

Ivanov who'd half risen from his chair, froze at the name. 'Leykin!' he couldn't help exclaiming. This must be the father of his poet friend.

'My name means something to you?' There was a menacing interest in the icy voice and Ivanov realised he'd slipped up badly.

He clutched at his head and murmured, 'Leykin, Leykin,' as though striving to grasp at a memory which eluded him. 'Poetry!' he exclaimed triumphantly,

'Leykin's a poet!' and then he added excitedly, 'Hold on, it's coming – I think I'm remembering something!'

Hesitantly he began to recite, his words coming singly at first, then tumbling out in a spate:

> *I am the verse*
> *You are the prosodist:*
> *Work out for me*
> *The measure of my time.*
> *You say:*
> *When time is done*
> *And you've become a speck*
> *Of dust or whisp*
> *Of gas; when planets freeze*
> *And suns burn out;*
> *When anti-matter spins*
> *Its stygian holes*
> *And spews a void where once*
> *Were living worlds–*
> *Then tell yourself, oh zek,*
> *You're free again!*

Ivanov looked at the two men. Khustov was beaming at him and nodding happily. 'You're beginning to remember!' he declared gleefully.

The colonel said nothing. His swarthy face had gone a parchment yellow and the scar stood out on his cheek like a fresh weal. He fumbled for the edge of the table to steady himself, staring unblinkingly at Ivanov. There was nothing baleful in the stare – no malice, no menace. The eyes were glazed with shock.

But next moment he'd recovered and when Khustov turned to him he was even smiling and nodding his head thoughtfully. 'Very promising,' he said to the lieutenant. 'Keep trying,' he said to Ivanov. With that he marched briskly out of the room, his heels rapping the floor, his back ramrod stiff.

42

Three days went by before Ivanov saw the colonel again. Meanwhile Khustov continued his interrogation and Ivanov continued to lead him astray. Whenever the young lieutenant faltered and ground to a halt before the blank wall of Ivanov's 'amnesia', Ivanov obligingly 'recalled' an odd fact which would send him off on another false trail.

It was like a draghunt with Ivanov laying a scent which took the poor lieutenant round in a circle. Ivanov wasn't doing it to frustrate Khustov; he was trying to put off the evil day when sinister Colonel Leykin would take over.

Ivanov didn't sleep well the night Khustov told him Colonel Leykin wanted to see him in the morning. Though he'd resigned himself to eventual defeat with the arrival of his prints from the regional bureau in his Don homeland, he wanted to carry his deception to the limit. It would be some recompense to know that he'd survived a KGB inquisition and had led them by the nose. But Leykin was no Khustov; this was going to be the ultimate challenge.

It was a sunny morning and warm for October but the colonel had a fire roaring in his stove. He greeted Ivanov amiably enough when Khustov escorted him into the room and invited him to be seated. Then he told the lieutenant to get out. His amiability had dropped like a mask.

'And make sure nobody disturbs us – nobody, not on any account, d'you understand?' he bawled at Khustov. The lieutenant glanced anxiously at Ivanov before he withdrew.

'Neatly done,' thought Ivanov, bracing himself for the ordeal to come, 'if I can stick this out I'll be shuttled back into the kindly arms of Khustov tomorrow.'

But there was no immediate outburst. The colonel left his desk and stood with his back to the stove, his hands clasped behind him. He was watching Ivanov closely, his head tilted to one side. Like a bird, thought Ivanov – a bird of prey sizing up its next meal.

'That piece of verse,' the colonel said quietly, 'that poem you recited the other day, strange you should know it – unless of course you knew the poet.'

Ivanov said nothing. No sound reached them from outside and the ticking of a clock on the colonel's desk became clamorous in the silence.

'That particular poem was never published,' Leykin went on, 'it wasn't even passed around in manuscript form. So the poet must have shown it to you himself – or given you a copy.'

Ivanov groaned inwardly. The colonel was right: Ilya Leykin had indeed given him a copy. But he wasn't going to admit it. Even though the colonel might be on to him he'd play the game out to the bitter end.

'If I may say so,' he said smoothly, 'I find your interest in poetry refreshing – even commendable in a KGB officer.'

Leykin smiled thinly. 'You're a cool customer. You know of course that Ilya was my son.'

'*Was?*' exclaimed Ivanov.

'You didn't know? Of course not. You'd have no way of knowing where you've been for the last few years.'

The colonel walked slowly from the stove back to his desk. The crispness had gone from his stride. 'He died in a labour camp just over a year ago, TB they told me.'

'I'm sorry,' said Ivanov, and when Leykin looked up to meet his gaze he added, 'and I mean that.'

'I know you do,' said Leykin, 'when Ilya made friends he made them for life.'

Ivanov said nothing. Was the colonel using the death of his son to get him to talk? He didn't think so. No man could stoop so low, not if he'd loved his son.

'Awkward for me, isn't it?' the colonel said, as though he'd been reading Ivanov's mind, 'but I know where my duty lies, so – back to business!'

He opened a drawer in his desk and placed four folders on the desk top, lining them up neatly. Two of the folders were thin, two thick.

'No need to say a word, these files say it for you.' Leykin shook his head ruefully and smiled almost apologetically at Ivanov. 'It was so simple. I knew when – and most important where my son had written those lines you were so indiscreet as to quote to us. All I had to do was check your fingerprints with just one regional records bureau – the one covering the Don area. And they sent me this.' He picked up the thinnest of the folders. 'The civil dossier of Ivan Mikailovitch Ivanov.'

Ivanov winced at the sound of his name. This was the moment he'd dreaded ever since the madcap scheme to lose his identity first possessed him in the taiga. He was surprised he wasn't more upset.

'I then sent off for your military dossier.' Leykin picked up the other slender folder. 'You were a good soldier,' he said approvingly, 'I see your commanding officer thought highly of you.'

Ivanov managed a stiff nod to acknowledge the compliment. He felt more like saying, 'So what?' Nothing could save him now, not even a character reference from the Kremlin.

Finally Leykin reached across the desk for the remaining files. They were so bulky he had to use both hands. 'And of course these,' he said, raising and lowering the files as though to demonstrate their weight, 'these are your

prison records and our KGB dossier on you. Two
quite hefty volumes, you must agree.'

Leykin leant back in his swivel chair and swung away
from the desk with the air of a man who had finished with
something thoroughly distasteful. Ivanov had his eyes on
the floor, but he didn't see the polished boards, the
Bukhara rug with its tasselled corners. He was looking
down into the black abyss of the years to come.

They'd never let him go, not now. He'd end his days in
a labour camp, worn out by toil and hunger. He'd never
again see Katerina and Alyosha, and in time his mind,
clouded by the anguish of his breaking body, would lose
all memory of them.

The ticking of the colonel's clock filled the room again
and Ivanov seized on the sound as though to hold on to
time itself. Tick-tock, tick-tock! He felt his heart was
breaking.

43

'It was a good try. You certainly put us off the scent with
Jablonsky's movement order.' The colonel's voice came
to Ivanov as from a great distance.

'And you did the amnesia bit very convincingly too.
Our psychiatrist has swallowed it hook, line and sinker.'
Leykin chuckled. 'Pity in a way he'll never know. I like
taking those head shrinkers down a peg or two when I get
the chance.'

Ivanov looked up. Wasn't Leykin going to tell the
psychiatrist? But the colonel, who had swung his chair
round to face the window, seemed to be speaking more to
himself than to Ivanov.

'You must have had a tough time in the taiga, and

although I'm only guessing, I'd say you stumbled on the wreckage of that plane quite by accident. That's how you picked up the dioxin poisoning – another real puzzler for us. But I suppose the plane in some way also helped you through the winter. I don't know how and in fact I don't want to know. The less I know the better for me – and for you....'

The colonel's voice trailed off and Ivanov straightened in his chair, his gloom of a moment before gone in a sudden blaze of hope. Had he heard aright? Was the colonel hinting at a way out? No, it couldn't be; Leykin might be Ilya's father but he was first and foremost an officer of the KGB. He'd already said he knew where his duty lay.

'What baffles me is how you intended dealing with your prints.' The colonel had started talking again, in the same thoughtful, speculative tone. 'You must have known all along that fingerprints would find you out. Even if your civilian and army records went astray it would only have been a matter of time before somebody thought of running your prints through our KGB system. I'm surprised in fact that Khustov, slow as he is, hasn't already thought of it.'

Ivanov dared a question. 'D'you mean Khustov still doesn't know who I am?'

Leykin swung his chair round to face Ivanov. 'Only I know.' He was looking steadily into Ivanov's eyes. 'And as I said before I know where my duty lies.'

He leant across the desk and swept the files into a bundle. 'My duty is to the memory of my son.' He carried the bundle over to the stove and turned again to Ivanov. 'You were my son's friend and you went to prison for him.'

Leykin opened the lid of the stove and fed the papers from the files one by one into the flames. Ivanov watched him as though in a dream, not yet fully grasping what was being done.

'Nobody here knows I sent for the dossiers,' said Leykin as he crumpled up the empty folders and thrust these too into the stove, 'and there are no copies anywhere, I made sure of that.'

Ivanov tried to speak but sudden tears choked his words. Leykin glanced at him and then looked away hurriedly, making a show of fussing with the lid of the stove. When the lid clanged shut he stole another glance at Ivanov and tapped on the stove with the poker, grinning like a schoolboy. 'And there goes Ivan Mikailovitch Ivanov,' he proclaimed theatrically, 'he never existed because there's not a scrap of paper to prove he ever did!'

Ivanov smiled through his tears and then buried his face in his hands. He'd been resolute enough when alone and with all the odds stacked against him; he'd have died rather than be seen to weep. But now that he had a friend and a real promise of freedom his defences crumbled.

He felt Leykin at his side and a hand gripped his shoulder firmly. 'Let yourself go,' said the colonel, 'there's no shame in it for a man like you.' The harsh voice softened. 'You've held on long enough and it's all over now.'

Ivanov blinked away his tears. 'You mean I'm free?'

'Not only free, but a new man.' The colonel walked to the door and opened it. 'Khustov!' he bellowed, 'some brandy and water! Our friend here is sorely in need of it.'

Khustov appeared in the doorway and looked in dismay at the huddled figure of Ivanov. Sudden anger flashed in his blue eyes. 'Comrade Colonel, there was no need to–'

'I said brandy and water,' interrupted Leykin harshly, 'and keep whatever you've got to say for later. I haven't finished with the man yet.'

Leykin stalked back to his desk and sat rigidly upright in the swivel chair until the orderly who brought in the brandy and water had closed the door behind him. Then he sat back and smiled reassuringly at Ivanov.

'That was for Khustov's benefit. I want him to believe I'm giving you a real grilling.' He filled a glass from the brandy bottle and pushed it over the desk to Ivanov. 'But in any case you can do with a drop of this.'

<h1 style="text-align:center">44</h1>

Ivanov was glad of the brandy. It calmed him. He'd felt he was losing touch with reality but now found he could listen to the colonel without wanting to pinch himself to make sure he wasn't dreaming.

'I'll have to confess defeat to Khustov,' Leykin was saying, 'and tell him that hard as I've tried I can't ferret out any sinister design or any motive which could make you want to deceive us. I'll say you're harmless.'

Then he'd go through the motions of deciding what to do. Fortunately Khustov had already suggested that if Ivanov was in the clear they should give him a new identity and let him go. Leykin intended to allow the young lieutenant to persuade him to take this course.

'So you can see, my final decision will follow our line of thought,' said the colonel, 'it won't strike a jarring note.'

He swung round in his chair yet again to face the window and nodded at a glimpse of blue sky and wooded hillside. 'But your mind's out there now, eh?' he said. 'You've a new life to plan, new work to do, a new home to make.' He sounded envious. 'And don't worry about your wife and child. Once you've settled on what you want to do and where you want to live I'll see that they join you.'

Ivanov gulped down what was left of his brandy and almost choked. 'I don't know what to say,' he spluttered, 'how can I ever thank you? The trouble you're taking – and the risk you're running. Why, they'd shoot you if anybody found out!'

'No risk,' said Leykin, and he gave an ironic little bow, 'thanks to you. You've prepared the ground so well with your own tale that all I'm doing is capping it.'

'But those dossiers you've destroyed,' protested Ivanov, 'won't the people who sent them to you want them back?'

'I'll tell them I've lost them.' Seeing Ivanov remained unconvinced Leykin added reprovingly, 'You know, I'm not exactly a beginner in frolics of this sort. I've helped people before and run worse risks than this.'

'Sorry,' murmured Ivanov, 'I thought it was because of Ilya—'

'Certainly because of Ilya,' interrupted Leykin, 'your friendship with him made it my duty to help you. But even before I knew who you were I'd decided to take you under my wing.'

He smiled at the bewildered Ivanov. 'Sorry to disillusion you – and I suppose it's professional pride which makes me say it – but right from the start, when I first learnt of your arrival at Ignayetsk, I was on to you. I had no idea what you were up to, but I did know you were bucking the system and that was good enough for me. That's when I decided you were yet another who needed a helping hand.'

'Another?' asked Ivanov, 'there've been many others?'

Leykin nodded. 'And I'll tell you why.' He looked about him, at the room and its furnishings, and shrugged disdainfully. 'I don't belong here, I'm an army man. They got me into the KGB under false pretences – to inject some military discipline into the system, they told me. But I soon realised they only wanted me for my specialist knowledge. At the time they were rounding up returned prisoners of war and my job was to screen them. All the lads who passed through my hands I cleared for a return home only to discover later they'd been packed off to Siberia. That did it. From then on the KGB became the enemy for me and their victims became my friends. Then they arrested me, but not for helping people get away from the KGB. Oh no, they'd no idea what I was doing. My crime was simply being the father of Ilya Leykin, the dissident poet, and that got me four years in a labour camp. Of course when Stalin died they blamed it on him and wanted to make it up with me by inviting me back into the KGB. I jumped at the chance of coming back – and there's no need for me to tell you why, is there?'

'Positively no need!' replied Ivanov warmly. Then he added quietly, 'Did Ilya know? Did you tell him all this when he came to see you just before they took him away for the last time?'

Leykin looked down. For once he seemed to be avoiding Ivanov's eyes. 'I haven't thanked you for that visit,' he said evasively. 'Ilya told me it was you who'd persuaded him to come – much against his better judgement, I think he said. But thanks to you I did at least see him.'

'But did you tell him?' persisted Ivanov gently, 'did you tell him you were helping others?'

Leykin shook his head. He looked suddenly old and tired. Deep lines which had appeared round his mouth seemed to be tugging at the livid scar on his cheek as though to open the old wound.

'I couldn't.' His voice was no more than a whisper. 'The boy had enough on his mind and I didn't want to saddle him with my secret as well. It would have been too much of a burden for him.'

Ivanov drew a deep breath. He felt he'd touched something exquisitely tender deep down inside this strange man. For all his tetchy toughness, his military swagger and cocksure airs, for all his courage in risking his life to help others, he was as helplessly fragile as any other father who'd been rejected by his son.

'I'd like you to think of me as a friend,' said Ivanov quietly. 'You must come to see us, you must meet Katerina and Alyosha.'

Leykin shook his head. 'Too risky for you and for them.

I mustn't kid myself I can play this sort of double game for ever. Sooner or later somebody's bound to smell a rat, then I'll be for the high jump – and so will everybody I've been friendly with.' He nodded towards the door. 'Take young Khustov out there, I like that lad but I've got to treat him like dirt to make sure he doesn't get chopped down with me. Friends are a luxury I can't afford.'

A deep compassion for Leykin stirred in Ivanov and with it came the startling thought that for the first time since his arrest he wasn't thinking of himself. Day in day out he'd striven to find a way to freedom – but only his own freedom; night after night he'd dreamed of happiness – but a happiness which could be shared only with Katerina and Alyosha. Yet now he was moved by the plight of a man who'd never figured in his scheming and his dreaming.

It was then – and only then – that Ivanov knew he was free. He'd been blinkered by his obsessive bid for freedom, seeing only his own road ahead. Now he could see the millions plodding at his side, not just *zeks* like him but men like Leykin, prisoners too – prisoners of the system. And he could not only see them; he could feel for them.

Ivanov knew he was at last truly free.

EPILOGUE

In the little town of Perenskaya on the wooded shores of Lake Chukhloma there is a forestry college. Its principal is Sergei Fyodorovitch Golyakov, who joined the college as a student teacher fresh from the University of Moscow.

When he arrived he was old for a student. 'I'm a late developer,' he joked. And perhaps after all there was something immature about him, thought the local gossips, for instead of picking out a bride for himself from among the many eligible young ladies of the town, he chose to marry a widow with a young son who'd arrived in Perenskaya only a few weeks before him.

Golyakov was a brilliant teacher. When he talked about trees he made them live and breathe in the imagination of his listeners, and his knowledge of woodcraft held his students spellbound. Little wonder he was swiftly promoted – to the satisfaction of the worthy citizens of Perenskaya, it should be said, for they knew a good man when they saw one.

But they wouldn't have been so sure had they seen their respected college principal working late at night behind the locked doors of the photo-copying room, knee deep in banned works – novels, verse, essays, histories. For Golyakov's secret vice was copying. In fact he ran the biggest copying centre in the *samizdat* network – the system which enables Russians to read in manuscript form what their masters have decided is bad for them.

Golyakov had no literary pretensions himself and succumbed only once to the temptations of authorship. That was to produce a thoughtful monograph on the life and works of Ilya Aleksandrovitch Leykin, one of Russia's lesser poets. He dedicated his slender opus to the poet's father, a certain Colonel Aleksandr Nikolayevitch Leykin, whose name would otherwise not be recorded anywhere. He was shot by the KGB and people who end their lives that way don't get an obituary.

Golyakov's son, by the way – they thought it would be nice for his wife's Alyosha to have a brother – the son is called Aleksandr.

ABOUT THE AUTHOR

While still a boy, Russell Evans sought the road to high adventure the classical way – by stowing himself aboard a ship. But it had steam up for moving only from one dock to another and didn't leave port! On finishing school he tried again, but this time by getting a job as cabin boy on a tramp shipping wheat from Russia's Black Sea ports. This was at the height of the muzhik famine when every bushel of grain exported could have saved a peasant's life. The experience left him hating dictatorships and admiring the astonishing fortitude of people who have to endure them.

After training as a newspaper reporter, he volunteered to fight for the Republicans in the Spanish Civil War, only to end up being grilled by a kangaroo court in Red Montmartre on suspicion of being a Franco spy. Disillusioned, he left for South America on a madcap scheme for starting a new republic in a remote corner of Amazonia. Two years later he emerged from the wilderness to find Hitler's war had started and hurried home. He fought in Wavell's Western Desert campaign, including the siege of Tobruk, was rescued from a sinking destroyer, took part in the Sicily landings, then served in Italy and finally in the Far East. He was a captain in the Intelligence Corps, and one of his earliest assignments was frontier control work in Egypt with the late Maurice Oldfield who was to become, as chief of MI6, Britain's top spymaster.

After the war Russell Evans returned to South America for a final adventure before marrying and settling down to the more predictable life of a newspaper reporter. For fifteen years he was editor of a county weekly in mid Wales and then taught journalism in Cardiff College of Commerce. Now he works from home, writing. His wife is a doctor and they have one son.

THE MOTORCYCLING BOOK
John Dyson

A complete guide to motorcycles and mopeds for the inexperienced rider, giving information on the kinds of bikes available, what to look for when you are buying for the first time, and expert advice about staying alive on the road. Essential reading for anyone who owns or wants to own a two-wheeler.

KNOW YOUR BODY
Dorothy Baldwin

A witty, helpful guide to matters of health for young people. A book for browsing through, laid out in alphabetical order, and designed to help understand the mental and physical changes which occur during the teens.

NOAH'S CASTLE
John Rowe Townsend

Set in a lawless, hungry Britain, this provocative book paints a chilling picture of a family under stress, revealing their strengths and their weaknesses. Recently filmed for television.

A VERY LONG WAY FROM ANYWHERE ELSE
Ursula Le Guin

A very contemporary problem. Owen has difficulty coming to terms with a real relationship because of the teenage media's concentration on sex.

THE TWELFTH DAY OF JULY
ACROSS THE BARRICADES
INTO EXILE
A PROPER PLACE
HOSTAGES TO FORTUNE
Joan Lingard

A series of novels about modern Belfast which highlight the problems of the troubles there in the story of Protestant Sadie and Catholic Kevin which even an 'escape' to England fails to solve.

THE ENDLESS STEPPE
Esther Hautzig

The exile of a young child and her family to Siberia and their subsequent life there. This magnificent and moving book is a true story which will live long in the memory of any reader.

PROVE YOURSELF A HERO
K. M. Peyton

Kidnapping is a terrifying enough experience itself, but Jonathan finds that his eventual release causes him even greater problems!

THE KING OF THE BARBAREENS
Janet Hitchman

True story of an orphan, a plain, intelligent girl who is passed from one foster-home to another. She longs for love but ruins her chances by her defiant attitude.

SOME PENGUIN BOOKS YOU MIGHT ENJOY